"A magical adventure that will touch your heart and tickle your funny bone. I loved it."
Maz Evans, author of WHO LET THE GODS OUT

"The new Worst Witch! Full of charm and chuckles. Kids are going to LOVE it."
Abi Elphinstone, author of JUNGLEDROP

"A brilliant, hilarious story!"
Emma Carroll, author of LETTERS FROM THE LIGHTHOUSE

"Love, love, loved it! It made me smile the whole way through!"
Jennifer Killick, author of CRATER LAKE

"Super sparky, funny and brimming with magic and imagination."
Andy Shepherd, author of THE BOY WHO GREW DRAGONS

"Positively fizzes with magic and genius imagination."
Rachel Morrison, author of HOW TO GROW A UNICORN

"Brimming with magical mishaps and sprinkled in humour, this book completely charmed me."
Jo Clarke, author of LIBBY AND THE PARISIAN PUZZLE

"Such a lively, playful and hilarious caper! Diary of an Accidental Witch has a classic feel with modern twists and a catchy style."
Kate Foster, author of PAWS

TO LITTLE WITCHES EVERYWHERE, THIS ONE
IS FOR YOU, H AND P xx

FOR ARCHIE AND OLIVE, MY LOCKDOWN
HEROES, LOVE MUM x

STRIPES PUBLISHING LIMITED
An imprint of the Little Tiger Group
1 Coda Studios, 189 Munster Road, London SW6 6AW

Imported into the EEA by Penguin Random House Ireland,
Morrison Chambers, 32 Nassau Street, Dublin D02 YH68

A paperback original
First published in Great Britain in 2021

Text copyright © Perdita & Honor Cargill, 2021
Illustration copyright © Katie Saunders, 2021

ISBN: 978-1-78895-338-2

A CIP catalogue record for this book is available from the British Library.

Printed and bound in the UK.

MIX
Paper from
responsible sources
FSC® C020471

The Forest Stewardship Council® (FSC®) is a global, not-for-profit
organization dedicated to the promotion of responsible forest management
worldwide. FSC defines standards based on agreed principles for responsible
forest stewardship that are supported by environmental, social, and
economic stakeholders. To learn more, visit www.fsc.org

10 9 8 7 6 5 4 3 2 1

Diary of an ACCIDENTAL WITCH

PERDITA & HONOR CARGILL
ILLUSTRATED BY KATIE SAUNDERS

LITTLE TIGER

LONDON

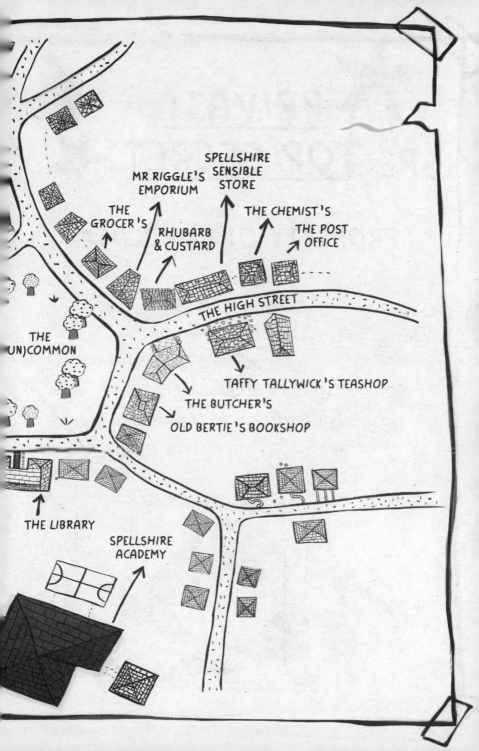

PRIVATE
TOP SECRET

PROPERTY OF BEA BLACK

1 Piggoty Lane,
Little Spellshire,
Spellshire,
Back of Beyond,
Far, far from civilization...

MONDAY 13TH SEPTEMBER

5:20pm Home

It's our first full day in Little Spellshire and Dad has given me this diary to 'celebrate' moving. I know a bribe when I see one – he might be 'celebrating', but I never wanted to move here. It's quite disappointing how little my opinions count in this family. Who decides to move somewhere just because it's got *funny clouds*? Only my dad, that's who.

On the upside, a bribe's a bribe and I've wanted my own diary since I was in Year Three and Milly Strudel had one that smelled of strawberries. This one doesn't smell of anything except new paper, but it's still really nice. I'm going to write down everything that happens to me and I'm never going to miss a day.

5:43pm

Except ... probably NOTHING will happen to me because now I'm literally living in the middle of nowhere and there's NO RELIABLE PHONE SIGNAL and I haven't got any friends. I suppose that means I'll have time to faithfully record all my ~~deep~~ thoughts.

Things I Will ACHIEVE This Year Now I Have No Friends

- Become a world-famous diarist (must look up other world-famous diarists so I can copy how they do it).
- ~~Learn to speak fluent Italian, Mandarin and possibly Japanese.~~ (Too tricky.)
- Master all the trickiest football skills, especially the Seal Dribble and the Hocus-Pocus.
- ~~Learn to play the piano.~~ (WAY too tricky!)
- Persuade Dad to let me have a puppy.

6:11pm

I HAVE A FRIEND! Well, hopefully...

He's called Ashkan (but he says everyone calls him Ash except his mum). He lives next door and, even though his mum had obviously dragged him over to be neighbourly, he seems really nice. It was very sunny so we sat in the garden and had lemonade. Mrs Namdar wanted to know why we'd moved here and Dad explained that he was a weather scientist and was writing a book about Little Spellshire's famously freaky microclimate. Then they got on to schools – Ash is in Year Seven too – and they talked for AGES over our heads about how good Spellshire Academy is and how it's much better than the other school in town *blah blah blah*.

When they finally drew breath, Ash said he'd show me round the **Academy** after school tomorrow if I wanted (yes!) and asked if I like cakes (YES!). Then he went to his house and came back with a plate piled

with little green cakes he and his mum had baked as
a Welcome-to-Piggoty-Lane treat for us.

Then there was a sudden and surprising
SNOWSTORM and we all had to run for cover.

6:30pm

It's stopped snowing, the sun is scorching again and
we're having the cakes for tea. **Yummy.**

TUESDAY 14TH SEPTEMBER

2:24pm Home

I've only got a few days of F R E E D O M

before it's back to English and History and MATHS,

eurgh! I'm not meeting Ash for ages, so I'm going to

explore Little Spellshire. From what I saw when we

drove through town the other day, it's nothing like

where we used to live. I asked Dad if I could go on

my own and he said of course I could because, if *I*

was ever going to turn out to be a scientist, the more

exploring I did the better. I was pretty sure I'd need

to be better at actual science to be a scientist, but I

didn't argue with him. NO IDEA what I want to 'turn

out to be' but exploring is one of my MOST favourite

things to do.

3:44pm Taffy Tallywick's Teashop

On the upside, I'm sitting writing this in a cosy teashop next to a fire with a little black kitten curled up on my lap. On the downside, unless this storm passes soon, I'm going to be seriously late meeting Ash.

I think it might have been a weeny bit of an understatement when I said Little Spellshire was nothing like where I used to live – it is very, EXCEEDINGLY, UNRECOGNIZABLY different.

For a start, it's **TINY**! Our house is at one end of Piggoty Lane and backs on to the path to the forest (that's my next place to explore), but at the other end – past lots of ordinary little houses like ours – the lane comes out on to a funny-shaped green all dotted with trees and pretty weeds called the Common – or

6

maybe the *Un*Common depending on which sign you
believe. There are hardly any people around and only
a few cars (mostly orange and bubble-
shaped for some strange reason),
but there are gazillions of CATS
– they're everywhere, curled
round street lamps, chilling on
postboxes and sleeping on the
steps of the library.

All around are thatched cottages and wiggly old shops. The shops are NOT what I was hoping for. Most of them are ordinary, if a bit old-fashioned – like the greengrocer's with its barrels of turnips and red apples outside and a butcher's with gross dead things hanging in the window. But a few are more ... *peculiar*, like MR RIGGLE'S EMPORIUM, which has a sign in its cloudy glass window saying *GET YOUR FRESH CUCKOO SPIT HERE!* I didn't go into Old Bertie's Bookshop because the old man peering at me from his perch on top of a teetering tower of cobwebby leather books scared me off and I obviously didn't go into the pub either (it's called The Moon & Broomstick and it's so covered in ivy that it looks like it's growing out of the ground).

Except for New Street, which is as straight as a ruler and lined mostly with modern houses, all the roads running off the UnCommon are twisty with more wonky old buildings. The Academy is at the end of New Street so I saved that one for later and checked out the High Street. **Spellshire's Sensible Store** sells boring stuff like beans and bacon and bin bags, and there's a chemist's with a sign saying REGULAR PRESCRIPTIONS ONLY and a neat display of nit treatments. But my favourite was Rhubarb & Custard because, as well as selling newspapers, it has SWEETS – a whole wall of them in big, old-fashioned, labelled jars.

Toffees

Chocolate eyeballs

Fizzy skullsquigglers*

Fluffmallows**

And I might have found a pet shop too. I could see a couple of owls sitting on a branch suspended from the ceiling and a handful of frogs hopping over the counter, but just as I was rattling the handle to see if it was open, the sky went black, there was a peal of thunder so loud several startled cats fell out of trees and it started to POUR with rain.

*Like jelly beans but much FIZZIER.
**Like marshmallows but much FLUFFIER.

"Quick! In here!" The door of the only tearoom on the street flew open and an arm reached out and pulled me inside. "You'll get soaked!"

Too late – I was already DRENCHED – but the arm belonged to Taffy and her tearoom turned out to be a very nice place to shelter. Especially when she brought me a hot chocolate and a big slice of millionaire's shortbread *for free*. She was very smiley and didn't do that *tut* thing because I wasn't grown up *and* she let me hang my coat and socks by the fireplace to dry out.

I've eaten all the shortbread, the kitten is purring and my socks are nearly dry, but it's still TIPPING it down.

4:13pm

Good news – it's finally stopped storming and, if I run fast, Ash might still be waiting at the Academy.

5:41pm Home

Just back from checking out MY NEW SCHOOL!

Unlike anything else I've seen in this place, the **Academy** is mega-modern, with lots of glass and steel and upbeat quotes about excellence stuck everywhere:

Believe To Achieve

In It For The Win

We Love League Tables, etc. etc. etc.

There are all-weather sports pitches that look AMAZING too! It's not as big as the secondary school I'd have gone to if we hadn't moved, but it's still sort of scary, especially because term's already started.

I told Ash I was nervous and he said he'd introduce me to all his friends. "You'll like it! It's just an ordinary school," he said, as if that was something to be very proud of.

I wanted to go and see the *other* school – the one called the School of Extraordinary Arts that I'd heard Mrs Namdar talking about – but Ash said we didn't have time because it's in the forest and it was getting late. It's true that the forest is very DARK and DEEP and TANGLY, but it's literally at the end of our gardens and it's not that late. I don't think that was Ash's only reason for not giving me a tour. He says the Academy is the only 'proper' school here and that I should forget about the other one. I don't know what he meant by that – maybe the schools have an epic rivalry like Arsenal and Spurs.

On the way home, I saw two more orange bubble cars with what looked like bright purple sparks coming out of their exhausts. Ash just shrugged and said I'd get used to it.

Odd.

7:32pm

Dad said Ash could stay for tea, but Ash had to go home and do his homework. It was probably for the best because tonight's menu was burnt sausages with a side of custard creams. Dad might know everything there is to know about thunder-snow, but he is a *disaster* in the kitchen.

Must add 'Learn to cook' to my list of **Things I Will ACHIEVE This Year Now I Have ~~No Friends~~ Only One Friend.**

SATURDAY 18ᵀᴴ SEPTEMBER

9:00pm Home

Missed a few days, but only because I ~~lost~~ ~~misplaced~~ tidied my diary in the bread bin.

Anyway, the only interesting thing that has happened to me in the last four days has been BAD.

I found out that I am NOT going to the Academy. I'm going to the OTHER school – the Extraordinary one stuck in the forest! And it's totally Dad's fault. All he had to do was register me at the library and he messed it up – he was so busy obsessing about peculiar precipitation* that he wrote my name in the *wrong book*.

"I'm sure the School of Extraordinary Arts is just as good," was what he said when he finally summoned up

*Or funny rain as normal people call it.

the courage to tell me what he'd done. "It'll be *fine*."

"But I don't even have ONE friend there," I wailed.

"You'll make friends." Dad made it sound like the easiest thing in the world. "And, until you do, you'll have more time for maths!" He laughed. I didn't. Instead, I ~~demanded~~ asked nicely that he UNregister me ASAP.

But, although he said he was sorry about a hundred times and looked as sheepish as an actual sheep *and* gave me the last fluffmallow in the house, apparently school transfers are tricky and the best he could do was promise to *try*. "But give it a good go first, Bea," he said hopefully. "Maybe it's fate..."

It's not FATE – it's a

DISASTER.

Maybe he'll feel so guilty he'll buy me a puppy.

SUNDAY 19TH SEPTEMBER (GOING-TO-NEW-SCHOOL EVE!)

11:43pm Home

I'm not asleep. Well, *obviously* I'm not because otherwise I couldn't be writing this but, more to the point, I'm too ~~scared~~ EXCITED to sleep. OK, I am a tiny bit scared, but that's because Ash came over earlier and went on and on in a not-at-all-reassuring way about how the *extraordinary* thing about the School of Extraordinary Arts was how WEIRD it was. I said it was just school and how strange could it be? And he said, "Have you seen the uniform?" and laugh-snorted so hard some of the Coke he was drinking came out of his nose.

Of course I've seen the uniform. I'm looking at it

right now – freshly ironed (Dad only burned through the fabric once) and folded up on the stool at the bottom of my bed. I don't hate it, but it's ... *distinctive*.

A purple pinafore so dark it looks almost black

A gold silk tie with fat black diagonal stripes

A white shirt with a starched collar – and, in my case, one very badly burnt cuff

Socks with bright gold-and-pink stripes (the Year Seven colours)

And – this is the bit I really do like – instead of a blazer we have a short, flippy cape – midnight-purple lined in gold silk with a long hood and little tassels that tie at the neck

Ash might think it's HILARIOUS, but he has a dressing gown covered in Daleks so I don't see why he's suddenly the authority on fashion.

MONDAY 20TH SEPTEMBER (AAAAAAAAAAARRGH!)

12:06am Home

TODAY'S THE DAY! I should probably go to sleep now.

1:56am

I should definitely go to sleep now...

What *are* Extraordinary Arts? I wish I was better at drawing.

2:12am

Just woke up, panicking that I'd overslept.

7:56am

How could Dad let me oversleep?!

8:13am

I don't know why I was up half the night,
worrying about school. I should have been
worrying about BREAKFAST. How can my
dad be a scientist and not know the difference
between salt and sugar? That's the kind
of detail that makes all the difference
to Good Luck Pancakes.

I tell him they're YUMMY and manage
to eat nearly a whole one so as not to hurt
his feelings. He says, "I'm sure you'll be FINE!"
about a hundred times so I don't think he's *that* sure.
"You'll find your feet in no time," he promises.

Talking of feet, the stripey socks look even brighter
this morning. I'm basically *glowing* from the knees
down. Then Dad asked me if I was OK walking to
school on my own on the first day and I said of
course I was because I knew he had an important
meeting with a snowflake specialist from Greenland,
and anyway all I had to do was follow the path that
started at the end of our garden. I'd be *fine*. Probably.

"I KNOW everything will go really well today," says Dad. Mmm, well, I guess it can't get worse than the pancakes.

9:09am School

I was WRONG.

I haven't even been to class and I'm already sitting outside the headmistress's office.

I think it might be because I squashed her cat.

I didn't mean to, *obviously*. I'm not EVIL, and it wasn't because I prefer dogs (which is something I'm going to have to keep quiet about because of Little Spellshire being the Cat Capital of the United Kingdom and possibly the world). It was a **Very Unfortunate Accident** and mostly the broom's fault.

I was already running late because of the whole sleeping in and suffering-through-the-pancakes thing and I was barely five minutes down the forest path when it suddenly got super foggy and I'd have got lost if I hadn't spotted a pair of capes flashing gold through the trees ahead. I followed them at double

20

speed past a swampy green pond, through a brambly patch and out into a clearing. The fog lifted as suddenly as it had dropped and I could see the school! It had tall, twisty chimneys and grey turrets like a castle! Huge iron gates were propped open by what looked like big PUMPKINS and more caped students in groups of twos and threes were streaming through.

Eeeek! I was only halfway up the drive when the loudest bell I'd ever heard shook one of the towers. I was pretty sure that meant I was LATE. I made a run for it and, if someone hadn't *left a broom right in the doorway*, I might have made it all the way to registration without a DISASTER.

But they *did* and I *didn't*.

Obviously, I tripped over it and skidded across the marble entrance hall.

"LOOK OUT!" someone yelled – I was heading straight for the lady at the reception desk! I quickly swerved and landed instead with a terrible **thump** on something *soft* ... that *yowled*...

I was too scared to look.

There was a hissing noise like air escaping out
of a balloon and then SILENCE (broken only by
nervous giggles and gasps from the *audience* of
other students). But, after a few seconds of extreme
and worrying FLATNESS, the little black cat –
because that's what I'd landed on – sort
of puffed back into three
dimensions, got up, gave me
a hard stare and walked away
with its tail in the air.

Phew! There was a smattering of
applause. But the receptionist (who was *extremely*
old and looked a bit like my grandad's tortoise if
it had been wearing a black frilly dress) was NOT
HAPPY.

"That's all this school needs," she said. "Another
one."

"Another what, Mrs Slater?" asked a boy in a cloak
that was about ten sizes too big.

"*Pupil,*" she replied in the sort of tone other
people would use for words like 'black widow spider'

or 'plague'. She came out from behind the desk to check that I, no, that the BROOM was OK. "Too many children," she muttered darkly, placing it in a very large cupboard full of other brooms. So many brooms! I guess it must be hard to keep this place tidy – even the entrance hall was three storeys high with a big fireplace and the sort of cobweb-decorated staircase that looked like it belonged in a ghost story.

I was trying to distract myself from the crisis-at-hand with a little daydream of sliding down the wiggly banisters when a tall girl about my age, wearing the neatest sports kit I've ever seen in my life, said snippily that, "Only a **toadbrain** wouldn't jump over a broom." Then she informed me that I'd *assaulted* the *headmistress's* cat and *now I'd be in for it* and laughed. And, sure enough, two minutes later Mrs Slater was telling a scary senior to show me to the headmistress's office...

So here I am.

In for it.

9:29am

Well, that was a lot better than I was expecting.
Turns out Ms Sparks, the headmistress, had only
sent for me because she wanted to say hello on my
first day! She said it must be very intimidating for
someone like me to come to a school like this. I said
– without specifically mentioning the squashing-her-
pet thing – that I'd certainly had a rocky start.

"We can't have that," she said, all twinkly, and gave
me a biscuit so of course I felt guilty and confessed.
But she just laughed and told me not to worry about
Zephyr because there was "more to her than meets
the eye". And the cat, who'd been staring at me in a
very judgey way from the top of a bookcase full of
ancient books, leaped down and settled smugly on
her mistress's shoulder.

It was a good thing I hadn't landed on Stan, said
Ms Sparks, because he had a tendency to be in
the wrong place at the wrong time and was quite
squishable. I asked her who Stan was, but she just
said I'd meet him very soon.

"I was surprised to see your name on our list," she went on, "but then I remembered meeting your father in the butcher's and having a most interesting conversation about the effect of thunderstorms on cheese and I expect that explains it." That explained nothing, but it did sound very like Dad.

Ms Sparks asked me lots of questions like, what was my favourite subject? (PE) and did I enjoy homework? ("Love it!" I fibbed). Then she told me I mustn't worry too much about my grandparents not having gone to this school – which was an odd thing to say because they've never left Milton Keynes.

"Whatever you might imagine, Bea, and no matter what some people want to believe," she said, "it's not all inherited, you know. No student walks in here knowing it all, no matter who their ancestors are, and, if you ask me, there's not much knowledge worth acquiring that doesn't take a good deal of hard work. No one's born brilliant at baking, are they?"

Judging from my last attempt to make brownies, probably not.

"And no one's born knowing their eight times table, are they?"

DEFINITELY not.

"HARD WORK AND FOCUS and you'll be flying in no time! Flying – hahaha! But remember: don't tell a soul. Those of us who know, *know* and those of them who don't, *can't*."

I nodded enthusiastically, but it was all very confusing.

"Excellent!" she said. "I'm glad we understand each other." I wasn't sure what to say because I did NOT understand her, so I admired her dress, which was covered in glittery gold stars, and she gave me another biscuit. Then she told me to wait right there while she went to get it for me – whatever 'it' was.

I'm back outside the headmistress's office and I am
SHOOK.

Ash was right. This place IS weird. Very, *extremely*,
EXTRAORDINARILY WEIRD.

'It' was a *wand*.

A WAND.

A real ... actual ...

WAND.

For ME.

I wouldn't have known that's what it was because
at first glance it looked a bit like a knobbly chopstick,
but Ms Sparks was VERY insistent that it WAS a wand
and she doesn't seem like the sort of headmistress
to joke about that sort of thing. Also, when I fell over
in shock, she pulled out *her* wand and *spelled me
upright again*!

"See!" she said with a grin.

I might be back on my feet, but my head's spinning
and I'm very NERVOUS and maybe I shouldn't be
writing any of this down because Ms Sparks said I

wasn't to tell ANYONE. But she's nipped back into her office to print me out a timetable so she can't see me and, anyway, do diaries even count? Maybe I could write in secret code?

I ɐM A M⋆TCH SCH⋆⋆L

Maybe not. For now, I'll just have to make sure nobody reads this. EVER. Anyway, I can't write any more because Ms Sparks is coming back and she's going to take me to my first lesson – Physics.

Did I say? I am in a state of **SHOCK**.

12:43pm

It's only lunchtime but I'm hiding in a broom cupboard with a frog. A LOT has happened.

"You'll have a head start," Ms Sparks had said on the way to the Physics classroom. "What with your father being a scientist."

I didn't tell her I'd inherited Dad's awkwardness, but not his good-at-science-y-ness.

"Most of Physics is quite straightforward, isn't it? What goes up must come down," she said, then she opened a classroom door, shouted "Good luck!" and *abandoned* me.

It was CHAOS.

I was staring into a big room with about twenty students sitting at desks while one student was being shouted at by a teacher to *get down*. So far, so ordinary, except that ... *the desks were at least a metre off the ground*! And that seemed to be the part of the lesson that was going WELL because the student everyone was shouting at was not just twice as high up as the others: he was *upside down* with his hair dripping some sort of blue goo on to the students below.

"Whoop! I'm JUGGLING!" he yelled. "*No hands!*" And I've got to admit what that boy could do upside down with five tennis balls and one frog was pretty amazing!

Suddenly upside-
down boy saw me
looking, said, "Cat Girl?", lost
concentration and he, the
desk, the balls and the frog all
lurched alarmingly downwards!
I let out a shriek just as the
teacher grabbed something off his
desk that looked very much like my
wand, muttered something I didn't catch
and, without anyone else seeming to move
a finger, the boy and everything else turned the right
way up again before floating gently to the ground.

"If you try that again, Puck Berry," said the teacher,
glaring at the boy, "it's detention. And I'll take Stan,
thank you very much." He scooped up the sad-looking
frog and marched in my direction.

By the time he got to me, he was all smiley,
holding out his hand and introducing himself as
Mr Muddy. He looked like a Physics teacher should,
in a mismatched three-piece suit and a flowing

white robe that I think was the witch equivalent of a lab coat.

"Everyone," Mr Muddy said as he popped Stan-the-frog on his head and clapped his hands. "Meet Bea Black – New Girl! Haven't had one of those for ages! *Such fun!*"

Twenty pairs of eyes swivelled in my direction.

"Introductions, everyone!" ordered Mr Muddy and immediately, on every desk, a name appeared scrawled in different handwriting and scrawled in *my* handwriting on the only empty desk in the room was MY name!

Even though I was nearly falling over with nerves, I could appreciate that this trick was not only useful but very cool. My place was in between a girl with very curly hair who – I peeked at her desk – was called Winnie and ... *oh no*, scary-sports-girl-who'd-called-me-a-**TOADBRAIN**, Blair. Mr Muddy made her move her cape off my chair, which she did EXTREMELY slowly and with maximum side-eye. Then, as I was awkwardly hesitating, the chair shot out, my bottom sort of *attached* itself to the seat like it was on magnets and with a *WHOOSH* I was tucked in!

"Ooopsy!" I said.

"Who says 'ooopsy'?" Blair asked Hunter, the boy sitting in front of her.

"Lame," he muttered. (He had a point: I'd never said that before in my life!)

"Oooopsy!" I found myself saying again as the chair rearranged me a little closer to the desk. Blair and Hunter and Izzi – the girl sitting on the other side of Blair – all sniggered.

"Wands out!" Before I even had time to get to my schoolbag, my wand (MY WAND?!) leaped into my hand. "Levitation one-o-one," called out Mr Muddy to a chorus of groans. "Every witch's entry-level skill – let's see what Bea can do."

What *could* Bea do? I ransacked my brain. Nope, not a single science fact that had anything to do with levitation (I wasn't even sure I knew what the word meant).

"Come on!" he encouraged me. "Use your wand skills – get something in the air."

All eyes were on me. Even my wand curled back like a cat's tail and *looked at me*.

"Just point it at something and, you know, tell it to go UP," muttered Winnie. As advice went, it was a bit vague, but it was all I had. I shook the wand back into a straight line and pointed it at an exercise book that was lying on my desk... Surprise, surprise, nothing happened. In the meantime, everyone else was getting bored and all around me random objects – textbooks, fluffy key rings, pens, a banana – were floating off

34

desks and into the air. It was very distracting.

"Come on, Bea-Black-New-Girl!" Mr Muddy fist-pumped the air in encouragement. *Oh dear.*

"Let your wand know who's boss," Winnie directed in a loud whisper.

I was not feeling boss-vibes, but I had to do something, so I desperately *willed* the wand to do as it was told. *Wait* ... I could feel something happening. It was a sort of quivering, like a sneeze that wouldn't happen. *Pleeeease*, I begged it, *pleeeease*. Finally, with a cross little jerk, it spat out a crackle of sparks, which on the upside was VERY SURPRISING AND MAGICAL, but on the downside...

"Fire!" yelled Puck.

He was not wrong. Not only was my face AFLAME with embarrassment, one of the flying textbooks had caught alight and was zooming round the classroom.

"Fire!" yelled student after student, ducking out of the way. There were now at least five flaming books and a strong smell of burning banana.

Mr Muddy swooshed his wand, said something I didn't understand ... and suddenly it was RAINING!

The fires were out, but I was DEAD with embarrassment. I was also quite damp. I'd have run away except I didn't think my chair would let me.

"Don't worry," said Winnie, towelling her hair with her cloak, "nerves always mess up magic. On my first day, I set fire to my eyebrows." I wasn't sure I believed her, but at least she was talking to me – most of the other students were giving me judgey looks as they collected their stuff.

I was the last one to leave the classroom and Mr Muddy (who, it turned out, was Year Seven's form teacher) had one last 'gift' for me. "Here, I'm putting

you on Stan rota until further notice." And, before
I had time to say anything, my hands were full of
clammy FROG. "I know he doesn't seem like much,
but he's quite a *consoling* frog."

Stan gave me a look that was something close to
DESPAIR.

Anyway, longest diary entry EVER, but now you*
know why I'm ~~hiding away~~ enjoying some alone-
with-a-frog time while everyone else has lunch.

1:11pm
Stan's started making a funny noise, more like a **bark**
than a **croak**. Maybe he's hungry. What do frogs
eat? Clearly, nothing in my lunch box. Please tell me
it's not ALIVE things.

2:48pm
Just got out of English.

When I say 'English', what I mean is Incantations
and the Language of Spells.

"It's not always enough just to wave your wand

---

* Have become one of those peculiar people who talk to their diaries.

at something," said Madam Binx, plucking a cobweb off the giant Venus flytrap sitting on her desk and picking up a little gold watering can. "That might work for basic UP-DOWN stuff like *levitation*, but for something more specific and creative, you need to strengthen the spell with the right WORDS." Everyone except me nodded, as if she was making perfect sense. "Who can give me an example of something that makes word spells stronger?"

"Rhymes!" Blair called out.

"Good answer!" replied Madam Binx, carefully replacing the cobweb on the freshly watered plant. "Now which one of you witches is going to come up with an original rhyming spell to start us off?" She was wasting her time looking at me. "Ordinary English will do."

"*On to shelves and into nooks!*" yelled a girl in the front row, pointing her wand at a HUGE, tottering pile of textbooks in the corner. "*With this spell, I tidy these BOOKS!*"

I ducked as a heavy pink volume flew past my ear

to land on the shelf behind me. *Aaaaaarrgh*, and again! In seconds, the pile was gone, all the books were back in their places and everyone (except the student who hadn't dodged in time and now had a bloody nose) was clapping. I clapped too, but very quietly because I didn't want to draw attention to myself.

"Excellent work, Amara," said Madam Binx approvingly and, with a single flick, a gold star swooshed out the end of her wand and hovered above the girl's head for a moment before exploding into a little shower of sparks and one gold-wrapped sweetie that landed perfectly in her outstretched hand! "Right, *focus-pocus*, class. I want each of you to come up with at least three words that rhyme with each of these." Madam Binx turned back to the old-fashioned blackboard and wrote:

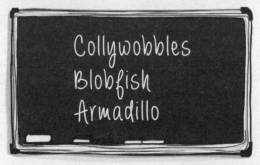

Collywobbles
Blobfish
Armadillo

Then she put down her pen, picked up her wand and with a "*Snip-snip-SNAP, feed my flyTRAP,*" magicked up a cloud of sparkly rainbow flying things for her pet plant!

I watched a twinkly blue bug land on the end of my pen and dissolve in a puff and ~~tried~~ FAILED to come up with something that rhymed with ARMADILLO. *Pocus-focus*, it was going to take more than some magic rhymes to calm me down today.

Polly-waffles?
Molly-coddles??
Slobwish?
Frogsquish??
Caterpillow???

2:50pm
According to Winnie Ross,* frogs eat FROG FOOD – available from Mrs Slater at reception. If I have any sense, she said, I won't ask what that is.

* Or Winnie Boss as Hunter calls her (I don't think he's being friendly).

2:51pm

The History teacher is off sick. Instead, "for a treat" (haha), Mr Muddy is going to give us an extra session of Physics. *Noooooooo...*

3:09pm

How long can I make this toilet break last?

3:13pm

When will this day end?

6:20pm Home

Dad's been home for exactly seven minutes (OK, eight now) and he hasn't stopped quizzing me on my day. "What are the teachers like? Did you meet the headmistress? Did you do well in class?" And, of course, the killer question, "Have you made any friends?"

I could barely speak after the day I'd had, but I managed to answer: "Yes, the teachers were OK", "Yes, the head was really nice but also a bit ...

unusual", **shrug** (because admitting that the only thing I'd managed to do was set the classroom on fire wasn't an option) and **SHRUG** (because I didn't want to tell him I hadn't made any friends because they all think I'm a **TOADBRAIN**).

Then Dad got all grumpy about me being "*uncommunicative*" and said he'd never have bought me a diary if he'd known I was going to spend more time "talking to it" than him, so I showed him my COMPLETELY NORMAL timetable.

Timetable: Year Seven (Form Teacher: Mr Muddy)
Student Name: BEA BLACK

Time	Monday	Tuesday	Wednesday	Thursday	Friday
09:00–09:15	Registration	Registration	Registration	Registration	Registration
09:20–10:00	Physics	Art	Chem/Biology	Chem/Biology	PE
10:05–10:50	Physics	Art	Maths	Zoology	PE
10:55–11:15	Break	Break	Break	Break	Break
11:20–12:00	Physics	Maths	English	Maths	Maths
12:05–13:05	Lunch	Lunch	Lunch	Lunch	Lunch
13:10–13:55	PD	PD	Whole School Assembly	PD	PD
14:00–14:45	English	English	Physics	History	Friday Lecture
14:50–15:30	History	Chem/Biology	Physics	English	Physics

NOTHING TO SEE HERE ↗

Dad asked me what PD (Personal Development) was, so I told him it was basically playtime (or what Mr Muddy had called "time to let your imagination go wild").

"Excellent, excellent!" said Dad, who very much approved of playtime – but then I didn't tell him I spent it all in a cupboard with a FROG. "And so much Physics!" He beamed.

8:02pm

Dad might be optimistic, but he's not stupid and it didn't take him long to go back to asking me if I was *sure* everything was OK. Everything was FINE, I ~~lied~~ said, but when we were washing up I reminded him of his promise to see if I could transfer to the **Academy**. He said he would, but then started talking to me in a Concerned-Parent Voice about Giving Things A Go and Facing New Challenges, so I fled to bed.

NEW CHALLENGES?!

He has no idea.

9:15pm

Ash is waving at me from his bedroom window.

"How. Did. It. Go?" he mouthed.

"A-MA-ZING," I mouthed back because that wasn't exactly a lie.

He opened the window and bellowed across, "Was it ... EXTRAORDINARY?" And then he snorted like he'd said something very funny. He has no idea.

I'm not going to open my window because I'm not really in the mood to chat.

I'm not even in the mood to write this **TOP-SECRET** diary. Which reminds me: must add 'Learn to write in code' to my list of

Things I Will ACHIEVE This Year Now I Have ~~No Friends~~ Only One Friend (and a frog).

9:37pm

C*D25 SI 4*RD

TERCES TON YREV??

EQFH HU JCTF!!

10:10pm

Abandoned attempts to learn code and spent an hour looking for a mega-safe hiding place for this

diary, but in the end have settled on my sock drawer. You could hide anything in there – it's very messy. My wand is still in my schoolbag because I'm too ~~scared~~ sensible to take it out. To be on the safe side, I've put the bag in my wardrobe and rammed a chair against the door. Should be FINE.

TUESDAY 21ST SEPTEMBER

1:45am Home

Woke up sweating. I had this *terrifying* nightmare that I'd gone to a school full of WITCHES and FROGS.

1:46am

Just checked the wardrobe. There *is* actually *a wand* in my schoolbag. So not a dream then...

8:13am

(*STILL Tuesday – I've been awake for hours.*)

　　Dad is feeling guilty because there are no eggs in the house and, according to an article he read yesterday in *Science Today*, my education is doomed unless I '*Go to School on an Egg*'. I don't think breakfast is my biggest problem. Anyway, it's not his fault; he was distracted by a Very Surprising MINI-TORNADO outside **Spellshire's Sensible Store** yesterday and came home with nothing more than one very large packet of pasta, three onions and a punnet of raspberries.

On the upside, raspberries for breakfast.

On the downside, no packed lunch. *Wait!* That might be an upside too...

11:14am School

Art is EXTRA-extraordinary at this school! Mr Zicasso wanted us all to "let our inner Da Vinciwick out". This was very tricky for me because I didn't know who or what Da Vinciwick *is*, but it involved a LOT of paint flying round the classroom and Puck was sent outside to stand in the corridor for drawing a big purple bat on Fabi's cloak. But no time to write

about it all now because, since I don't know how to SPELL my uniform clean like everyone else seems to, I've had to spend the whole of break in the toilets trying to scrub out the paint.

Stan is sulking – possibly because he is now more of a pink-and-blue frog than a muddy-green one. I tried telling him it was a good look, but he ignored me.

12:06pm

Very confused. I've just come out of Maths and there was something strange going on.

More to the point there *wasn't* anything strange going on.

We just sat there in near-silence and mastered fractions* under the stern gaze of Mr Smith who was wearing a grey suit with a not-even-stripey tie.

Where's magic when you need it?

12:10pm

No packed lunch means I'm going to have to brave

*I did NOT master fractions.

SCHOOL LUNCH and I'd rather face an army of flaming dragons (which, the way things are going, will probably be next week's challenge).

Obviously, it's not the actual *lunch* that's worrying me. I'm STARVING. But it's a lot easier to hide the fact I don't have any friends when I'm sitting in a cupboard with Stan, rather than sitting *on my own* at lunch with *no one to talk to*. I'm trying to look really busy writing this in the queue to go into the hall so nobody notices me. Maybe I could just ask a passing witch to invisibility spell me? NOT Puck.

12:21pm
Except ... *mmmmmm*, something smells good.

12:23pm
Sausages?

12:25pm

Winnie has come to tell me where to get my tray and cutlery – apparently, she's lunch monitor (she's monitor of just about everything) and ... she's asked me to come and sit with her and Puck and Fabi and Amara!

I think this is *good*?

12:28pm

Wow, this is NOT your average school canteen.
The QUEEN (if she didn't mind spiders) wouldn't look out of place in here. It's a huge room with wood-panelled walls dotted with old-fashioned portraits of important-looking people in black capes, and up front, laid out on a long, carved high table, there's literally a BANQUET! There are big, steaming ~~pots~~ cauldrons of some sort of stew and – my nose never lies – fat, sizzling *sausages* are cooking over a real open fire. And the pudding table is even better, with trifles nearly as tall as me, and CAKES, *so many cakes*! It's like Christmas but better because Dad's not cooking.

Things are finally looking up.

1:19pm

Things are no longer looking up.

I'd ~~greedily~~ enthusiastically heaped my plate with sausages (and some sprouts because the cook – who they all called Sir and who clearly wasn't someone to be argued with – had insisted) and squeezed on to the bench between Puck and Winnie, with Stan on my knee. Amara was having an argument across the table with Fabi about which of them should be captain of some PE team.

"Football?" I asked hopefully.

Fabi laughed and shook his head and when I asked what they did play – netball? Rounders? (anything with a ball would be fine by me) – he just grinned and said I'd find out. Then they started placing bets on who would score the most goals that term.

"It won't be either of you," said Winnie dismissively. "Blair always scores the highest."

I said she must be really good at sports and they all said yes, she was, and *very* COMPETITIVE. Cool. It didn't seem the moment to tell them I was very competitive too, so I changed the subject and said the first thing that came into my head – that I hadn't known boys could be witches.

Winnie was horrified. "That's so SEXIST," she said.

"And OLD-FASHIONED!" added Amara disapprovingly.

"But aren't boys *wizards*?" I ploughed on.

There was a sharp intake of breath.

"Wizards are something else *entirely*," said Puck.

They *were*? I had so many questions, but they

were all looking at me like they couldn't believe I didn't know what they were talking about, so I lost my nerve and focused on my sausages.

"Tuck in," said Winnie encouragingly, so I took an enormous bite...

BLLLEEEUUGH!

I *spat out* what was left in my mouth with such a lurch of disgust that Stan shot off my knee and flew halfway across the room. Oh no! All the witch students and one very large witch cook were staring at me.

"*Rude!*" loud-whispered Hunter from the next table. He had a point. I don't normally SPIT.

"B-but it tastes of—" I spluttered.

"Yes?" Scary Witch Cook was looming over our table like Dracula over a coffin. "*What* does it taste of?"

Er, not like any sausage I'd ever tasted. The closest I could get was inside-of-a-dog-basket-with-a-sprinkling-of-gherkin.

"It t-tastes s-surprising, S-Sir," I stuttered.

Blair, who was sitting next to Hunter, rolled her

eyes and chipped in with, "She's not used to OUR food, I suppose." She wasn't the only student tutting though – turns out witches, as a bunch, are a bit *judgmental*. Even Winnie, handing Stan back to me, looked disappointed. (Stan looked pretty horrified too, but maybe that was because he'd just been catapulted across the room and had landed on a teacher.)

Sir Scary Cook folded his arms across his huge chest and glared down at me. "Eat up," he said.

Everyone else was chomping away happily enough – maybe I'd just got a weird bit. Another look at Scary Cook persuaded me I had no choice. I took a second mouthful.

EEEEEEUGH!

This time I was getting definite hints of blue-cheese-with-cat-food. Little beads of sweat were breaking out on my forehead as I chewed.

"Well?" asked Scary Cook.

"D-Delicious," I managed, bright red with the effort of not spitting it out. What I would have given for one of Dad's salty pancakes. In the end, the only thing on my plate that was edible were the SPROUTS because they tasted like, well, *sprouts*. Things are bad when that's a win.

I think Winnie regretted asking me to sit at their table. Turns out witches are not just *judgey* but very easily OFFENDED.

3:01pm

So Chemistry is POTIONS and I'm not even surprised any more.

"What do you mean you haven't made a potion before?" asked Miss Lupo. Even after I'd explained I was new to Little Spellshire, she still couldn't get her head round it. "But surely you covered the basic concoctions at home?"

I had no idea what 'basic concoctions' were, but she looked so worried that I nodded.

"Well, that's a relief!" she said. "Goodness knows what would happen if you started making potions without knowing the basics! Hahahahaha!"

I wasn't laughing because I was too busy worrying about when we were going to find out.

"Spells aren't only about waving your wand or saying the right words – whatever the other teachers might tell you," she said. "Sometimes only a potion will do and that means learning about all the right ingredients and what to do with them."

Great. Another sort of magic for me to FAIL at.

Bear Breeches and Snapdragons, she wrote on the board, telling us to copy it in our exercise books. "Such an exciting combination!"

I'd ink-blotted my page so I tore it out, scrunched it up and, without thinking, lobbed it halfway across the classroom into the bin.

"Good shot!" called out Blair from right behind me, making me jump, and a second later not one but two balls of scrumpled paper flew over my head and landed perfectly in the basket.

That was a *great* shot ... but I could definitely do better. I was just about to attempt a TRIPLE when a voice said, "Bea Black and Blair Smith-Smythe! This is not a PE class." Miss Lupo was standing by my desk with a small, smoking cauldron in her hand. *Oops.*

"Now which one of you can tell me whether you would add one *tablespoon* or *half a teaspoon* of mucklespit to this recipe?"

Er ... not me.

Talking of recipes, I'm so hungry I could eat a horse.

3:03pm

Just seen a horse cantering past the window! OK, maybe not *that* hungry, but really VERY hungry-starving indeed.

I swear I can still taste those sausages. YEUK!

6:40pm Home

I ate every last mouthful of Dad's home-made mac'n'cheese, even though he'd forgotten to put in any cheese. "Yum!" I said.

He looked surprised.

"Can I have a second helping?"

He nearly fell off his chair. "That school is doing wonders for your appetite, Bea."

Dad looks tired. His book on *Understanding Little Spellshire's Most Peculiar Microclimate* is apparently "going nowhere". I know the feeling. My Maths homework is also going nowhere, unfortunately.

The unicorns at Zany Zoo are fed seven-tenths of a barrel of fluffmallows every day. The centaurs are fed half as many fluffmallows as the unicorns. How many barrels of fluffmallows are the centaurs fed in a week?

Seriously? All I know is that unicorns and centaurs should NOT be in a zoo.

I think the main reason Dad's upset is because

NEARLY

I'm not telling him anything. I used to talk to him about everything that happened at my last school. "But how is it *really* going?" he keeps asking, peering at me like I'm a particularly worrying cloud. I want to say that the only way it could be going *worse* would be if my Extraordinary School turned into an Extraordinary Boarding School, but instead I just mutter that I'm not sure I *fit in*.

"But it's good to stand out!" Dad says and I DESPAIR.

7:21pm

I waited until we were doing the washing-up and then asked Dad if he'd had any luck getting me transferred to the **Academy**. He looked guilty and told me to "leave it with him". That means he's forgotten.

I'm going to stick Post-it note reminders all over the house until he sorts this out.

8:11pm

Ash came over and we watched an old film about a scientist who'd shrunk his kids. Ash (who takes science very seriously) thought the plot was ridiculous, but I thought it was the sanest thing I'd seen all day.

Afterwards, Ash asked me lots of questions about school and got all grumpy when I wouldn't/*couldn't* answer. Then he told me the **Academy** was having a **Halloween** football match and I am so jealous I could SCREAM.

9:56pm

I wonder what makes wizards different to witches?

WEDNESDAY 22ND SEPTEMBER

10:32am School

Maths. Still haven't worked it out. When will the magic kick in?

I hope Dad's remembered to do something about GETTING ME OUT OF HERE.

12:37pm

Packed lunch in the broom cupboard with Stan again. I've never had raisin-and-tomato sandwiches before, but they're surprisingly OK. I wish I had some fluffmallows.

People keep saying words I don't understand so I think I'll go to the library now. I've got a long list of things I need to look up.

> [Extract from English Dictionary:]
>
> **Levitation,** *noun*
>
> The act of rising, or causing something to rise and hover in the air, typically by means of supposed magical powers.

What this library's missing is a helpful introductory manual on how to be a witch. Shame.

1:56pm

Survived my first assembly in the **Great Hall** (a room so ridiculously HUGE and GRAND it makes the dining room look ordinary), despite Ms Sparks pointing me out to the whole SCHOOL as the NEW GIRL. "Make sure you all give her an Extraordinary welcome!" she said.

I overheard Izzi mutter, "We sure will," to Blair who

was sitting next to her.

A couple of Year Nines who'd been sitting at the next table at lunch yesterday were pointing me out to their friends and I'd probably have burst with embarrassment there and then if it hadn't been for Ms Sparks's next announcement – the Halloween Costume Ball would take place on, *wait for it* ... HALLOWEEN. There was so much whooping I had to cover Stan's little ears.

"I expect everyone to make a splendid effort with their costumes this year," bellowed the head. "Applications for the Junior Ball Committee are to be made in writing to my office and if you want to be in with a chance of being crowned this year's Queen or King of Mischief (*more cheering*) write your name on a slip of paper and drop it into the cauldron by Mrs Slater's desk no later than going-home time this Friday!" The hall nearly exploded with excitement. I was surprised the noise didn't bring down the great, cow-sized, glittering chandelier that was hanging above our heads.

No one was talking about the New Girl any more.

2:01pm

I wonder what the Queen or King of Mischief does?

3:32pm

Why are witches so obsessed with making things go
up in the air? Especially things that really
should NOT go up.

Like frogs.

Or ME. Hunter might have
thought it was *hilarious* to
spell me from the bottom of
the Grand Staircase to the top,
but I didn't.

I am ~~TROMA TRAUMMATIZED~~
SHOOK.

8:15pm Home

Still too shook to write anything down so maybe I'll
start on my Physics homework.

> *Levitate three books of varied sizes – does an increased number of pages increase the difficulty of levitation? Record your results.*

Or maybe I'll just lie on my bed and feel sorry for myself instead.

THURSDAY 23RD SEPTEMBER

DAD TO DO:
Arrange for Bea
to MOVE SCHOOLS

FRIDAY 24TH SEPTEMBER

8:52am School

It's PE today. *Finally*, a lesson where I'll know what I'm doing. I've eaten three bananas for breakfast and I'm ready for anything.

New day, new me.

Upbeat-Bea-Me.

11:00am

I did NOT know what I was doing.

Everything seemed ordinary enough to start. I practically bounced out to the pitch in my new purple sports kit with my old trainers on. OK, so it might take a bit of time to get picked for a team, but this was a challenge I was up for.

The sports teacher, Ms Celery, looked normal – not a flowing cape in sight, just a plain tracksuit and a back-to-front baseball cap with WINNER written on it. "Snoozers are LOSERS!" she roared, sounding exactly like my last PE teacher. Happy days! "Come over here and collect your broomsticks."

And right there and then my upbeat mood melted away faster than a choc ice in a heatwave.

BROOMSTICKS.

Last time I'd encountered a broom, it hadn't turned out well and the stuff I knew now that I hadn't known then wasn't making me any more confident.

"Is ... there ... flying involved?" I asked.

Ms Celery looked at me like I was a bug (and she was one of those peculiar people that don't like bugs) and said, "*Obviously.*"

Great. So, instead of worrying about whether I'd get picked for a side, I should have been worrying about whether I might DIE.

"My skills are more *on the ground*—" I began but, before I could tell her just how good I was at dribbling, tackling and passing, she snapped at me to leave "that frog" in the changing room and get my BUTT out on the pitch. "MOVE IT, NEW GIRL!"

So I did, and a minute later I was standing in front of her, minus Stan, *quaking*.

"Do you know the rules of **GO**?" she barked.

Go? I'd have GONE *anywhere* at this point so long as it was on foot. I shook my head and she started shouting instructions at me so fast my head spun.

"OK, no time for the finer points of the game, just remember the BASICS – ten players a side, nine of them – the **GOers** – out on the pitch, the other one – the Sweep – indoors. The sole aim for the **GOers** is to get the ball into the goal using only their hands or the broom. Simple, right?" *Possssssibly* ... but, then again, probably not.

"Where are the goals?" I asked because the not-so-normal thing about the pitch (other than the two cats chilling in the middle) was that there didn't seem to be one.

"There," she said, pointing up.

"Where?" All I could see were the battlements of the school roofs and the twisty chimneys.

"*There*. To score you have to hit the ball down the chimney. *The Great* Chimney." Ms Celery jabbed her finger at the tallest, curliest one and told me it was a foul if the ball went down another one. So there really was ZERO chance of staying on the ground then? She juggled a ball the shape and colour of an orange and looked me up and down. "You, I think, are a Dodo." *Rude!*

"Try out as a **GOer** today." And she handed me
a neon-yellow bib and told me to put it on over my
kit.

Winnie, waving a clipboard,
came over and told me she was
the Sweep for the Dodos. "I have
to sit near the fire in the entrance
hall with the other team's Sweep,"
she explained. "If it's someone I
like, we gossip and if it's not I read
my book."

Normally, I'd have thought
that that sounded like the most
boring sports position EVER, but
right then, even if I'd had to read
our Maths textbook from cover to cover, I'd have
swapped with her. The Sweep's job was to record the
score when the ball rolled out of the fireplace. I asked
Winnie how she knew which team had scored and
she told me the ball changed colour. "Obviously."

Okkaaaaay.

Five minutes later, we were lined up, broomsticks in hand, in two witchy semicircles, the yellow DODOS and the bright red DRAGONS, facing each other on the pitch, and in the middle the cats (still chilling).

It was fast dawning on me that the game was about to start and *nobody had told me how to fly.* "Is it like riding a bike?" I whispered to Fabi, who was standing next to me.

"How would I know?" He shrugged, then peered at me and asked me if I was OK. "You look like you're going to be sick. Here..." He checked Ms Celery was too busy shouting at one of the Dragons to be watching, pulled a TINY pink stripey sock out of his hood and handed it to me. "My lucky sock," he explained. "It shrank in the wash, but it still works. You can borrow it." I had a feeling it was going to take more than a SOCK to keep me alive, but I stammered my thanks and stuck it in my pocket because I didn't know what else to do with it.

"And don't forget to be nice to your broom," Fabi called down.

Called down...

Everyone but me was now hovering metres up in the air!

"Oi! NEW GIRL!" bellowed Ms Celery. "Get that broom up NOW!"

I swung my leg over the broom and it seemed to come ALIVE! Maybe it was the teacher that made it happen, maybe it was the lucky sock, but ... I was *UP*! OK, I was wobbling and lurching, but I was *in the air*. Like a bird or a plane or an actual *witch*. And with Ms Celery shouting at me to "GO! GO! GO!", I *went*.

"Don't look down!" yelled Blair, who was captaining the Dragons. "Whatever you do, Bea Black, don't look down. Ha!"

So, *of course*, I looked down...

AAAAAAaaaaaarrGH!

I *crashed*. Over the next forty minutes, I *crashed* FIVE times, but ... I AM STILL ALIVE!!

That was not all. I also:

- threw the ball down the wrong chimney (one foul)
- threw the ball through the Year Eleven common-room window (one foul and possibly worse to come when they find out)
- collided with Puck mid-air – total accident (one foul)
- collided with Blair mid-air four times – the first two times were a total accident (four fouls, *not fair*)
- broom-grabbed Hunter – *sort of* an accident (one foul)
- was the VICTIM of no less than SIX fouls awarded against the Dragons – ha! – four of them from

Blair who is impressively aggressive in the air

- *wait for it* … SCORED a goal!!!!

Final score:

DODOS: 33   DRAGONS: 32

Take that, Achievement List! It was WILD.

Riding a broomstick is NOTHING like riding a bike.
It's absolutely BRILLIANT.

11:05am

I was coming out of the changing room with Stan
when I overheard Hunter telling Blair I was actually
"surprisingly good at **GO** for a **toadbrain**". I'd take that!

Blair said snippily that it wasn't fair to give me the
credit because Ms Celery had obviously given me a
super-enchanted broom that a Year One could have
stayed on and she'd still probably had to *spell me* the
whole way through the game.

"You're just worried she's better than you," said
Hunter.

Obviously, he was joking but, judging from her reply, Blair's not happy. Shame, because I was going to ask her how she managed to pull off a LOOP-THE-LOOP without falling off her broom. That's so going to the top of my **Things I Will ACHIEVE** list.

Look, maybe Blair's right and it was just the magic broom and beginner's luck, but *I don't care*. I've finally found something at the School of Extraordinary Arts I'm not HOPELESS at. Secretly feeling a tiny bit smug for the first time since I arrived in Little Spellshire.

11:15am

Nobody at this school knows how to ride a bike! Feeling SMUGGER.

12:02pm

Just got out of Maths. Not feeling smug any more.

3:35pm

I will never feel smug again. Physics was TORTURE.
Turns out that a) even when someone else has
levitated something up in the air, I can't make it
stay there (I honestly hadn't meant for the vase
of flowers to drop on Mr Muddy's toe) and b)
. the most important thing in wand-work
is keeping your wand pointed at the
thing or person you're enchanting (I
really hadn't meant to set fire to his
cloak).

"Magic on the loose," Mr Muddy
had said quite sternly, patting
down his cloak, "even beginner's magic, can be very
dangerous and unpredictable."

Oh dear.

7:56pm Home

I nearly blabbed to Dad when I got home – not
about Physics and Maths and being a **toadbrain**
obviously – but I was *bursting* to tell someone about

my GOAL. It turns out it's as hard not telling him
the good stuff as all the bad stuff but, as Ms Sparks
would say, "Those of us who know, *know* and those of
them who don't, *can't*," so instead I told him about the
Halloween Ball and then I wished I hadn't because he
got VERY enthusiastic.

"Can I make you a costume?" he asked and,
because he sounded like he really, really wanted to,
I agreed.

I'm not even *ten per*
cent confident in Dad's
needlework skills (the
last thing he 'sewed' for
me was a ghost costume
– AKA a sheet – and he
forgot I'd need holes for
my eyes), but WHAT
DOES IT MATTER?
By the time Halloween
comes round, I'll have
moved schools!

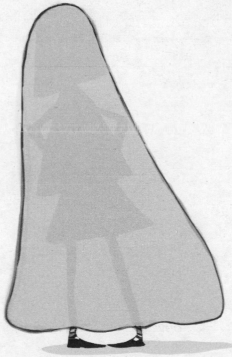

Pretty sure I won't have to worry about costumes at the **Academy**.

Cannot wait.

8:01pm

OK, I'll miss playing **GO**, but I won't miss anything else. I will especially not miss levitation and fractions and both sorts of spelling.

CANNOT WAIT.

SATURDAY 25TH SEPTEMBER

5:32pm Home

Well, that was AWKWARD.

Went to Rhubarb & Custard with Ash to stock up on skullsquigglers and fluffmallows, and bumped into Amara and Fabi who were buying out the shop's stock of purple twizzling sherbet. Ash stared at them like they were hungry tigers recently escaped from a zoo. To be fair, they did look a bit different out of uniform. Amara was wearing a dress that seemed to be made out of leaves and had pulled her braids up into a topknot studded with hundreds of tiny glittery cats. Fabi had accessorized his silver FLARES with a squashed top hat.

Before I could ask Fabi where he got the hat, three

of Ash's friends from school crashed through the door, setting off the creaky old bell hanging above it. They stopped short when they saw who else was in the shop. Everyone stared at everyone else and no one said a word. It was like some sort of military stand-off. The Extraordinaries on one side, the **Academy** kids (in jeans and hoodies) on the other. And I didn't know which group I belonged to! I *looked* like one of Ash's friends, I *was* one of Ash's friends, but also I was kind of, temporarily at least, an Extraordinary, and Fabi and Amara had never been mean to me. Also, I *really* liked Amara's dress.

In the end, I was so overwhelmed with awkwardness I accidentally spent all my pocket money on lime gazugglers and they are DISGUSTING.

"Why don't the people who go to your school talk to the people who go to my – the *other* school?" I asked Ash on the way home.

He shrugged and muttered something about the people who went to Extraordinary not talking to *them* and being super-secretive.

"You don't mind me though," I said and then pathetically asked, "do you?"

After a worrying pause, he said, "No." Then spoiled it by adding, "But you *are* secretive."

I wanted to deny it, but then I'd have had to tell him STUFF – and who knows what would happen to either of us if I did that? Ms Sparks would probably have to turn us into toads.

We walked the rest of the way home in silence.

I'm not sure if he's talking to me any more.

5:55pm

Ash just brought over some leftover cake. Nobody has
leftover cake (especially not when it's a super-sticky,
scrumptious spicy orange cake made by his mum)
so I think it's a peace offering. As a counter peace
offering, I asked him to stay and watch a Harry Potter
film with me.

8:32pm

He's just left and we're still friends. There was a
slightly awkward moment when he asked me if I
was taking notes during one of the scenes. I told him
not to be RIDICULOUS. (Of course I was.)

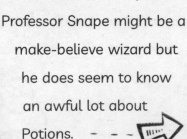

Professor Snape might be a
make-believe wizard but
he does seem to know
an awful lot about
Potions. - - - ➤

9:11pm

I must ask Amara where she got that dress.

10:01pm

I wonder if *I* could pull off silver flares?

SUNDAY 26TH SEPTEMBER

4:23pm Home

Spent the whole day shut up in my bedroom with my wand, trying to levitate things, LOTS of things – pyjamas, hairbrush, my bear, this book, this pen, etc. etc. No matter how hard I tried (very hard because, once you start trying to make things fly, it's quite hard to stop), nothing went so much as a micro-millimetre in the air. I thought my wand might be broken or need rebooting or something. I couldn't find any sort of ON/OFF switch though so I gave it a really hard shake, but all that happened was that I burned a hole in my pyjama bottoms. This magic stuff – *which I can't do* – is a serious fire hazard.

4:43pm

Dad just came up and asked for the millionth-zillionth time if I was OK and I said for the millionth-zillionth time that I was FINE. I was already feeling bad and then he started apologizing for the burn on my pyjamas. "I must have lost concentration when I was ironing," he said. "I was probably thinking about your costume for the ball."

I wasn't really listening because I was too busy trying to work out how to confess that I'd singed the pyjamas, without mentioning wands or getting into trouble about using matches, and then he said, "How about a *witch* costume?"

I GASPED.

"Great idea, right?"

TERRIBLE IDEA.

"I could whip up a long, ragged cloak and buy some stick-on *warts* and we could draw some hairs on your chin – turn you into a proper witchy witch."

RUDE.

"You'll need some stripey tights ... like your school socks, but red!"

What?! So I can offend everyone in the school – *especially red-stripey-sock-wearing Year TENS* – and the whole of the witching world? Has he no idea how SENSITIVE these people are?

"Oh." Dad stopped laughing and looked at me sadly. "You don't like that idea, do you?" *How could he tell??!* "OK, OK, I'll think of something else... I know, I'll make it a surprise."

I nodded weakly. I had NO WORDS.

Anything but a witch costume.

4:52pm

TO-DO LIST

- REMIND DAD TO HURRY UP AND GET ME MOVED SCHOOLS.
- Ask Blair how to do loop-the-loop on a broom.
- Find three words that rhyme with armadillo – karmadillo? Llamadillo??
- Learn to cook.

Maybe not. Too scary.

- REMIND DAD AGAIN TO HURRY UP AND GET
  ME TRANSFERRED TO THE **ACADEMY** *BEFORE*
  HALLOWEEN.

5:01pm

Right. I'm going to go downstairs and be the PERFECT
DAUGHTER and help with everything and TIDY the
kitchen, *then* I'm going to nag Dad about moving
schools.

5:41pm

What I would give for a tidying-up spell right now.
Talking of spells, our English homework is to write a
poem about the moon because Madam Binx says
a) all poems are magical and there's nothing better
for setting the scene for successful magic and b)
everyone knows lunar spirits especially enjoy poetry.

8:33pm

Still haven't ~~started~~ finished my homework. I'm not
sure what sort of poem a lunar spirit would enjoy.

12:07pm School

Bumped into Ms Sparks after Physics. She asked me how everything was going with a look of deep concern (possibly because my tie was on fire).

"Rr-r-really well," I stuttered, patting out the flames.

Ms Sparks fixed me with a Piercing Look and asked me how it was *really* going. I confessed that levitation was not coming naturally and she told me not to be disheartened because the only way was UP. I felt a bit better. "And at least you've got nothing to worry about in Maths," she added. "No levitation going on in Mr Smith's classroom."

I didn't feel better any more.

1:10pm

Blair's name was pulled out of Mrs Slater's cauldron after lunch today and she's going to be the Queen of Mischief at the Halloween Ball! She's pretty smug about it. Puck says it's a BIG DEAL and it's been a witch tradition since the days of Minerva Moon (whoever she is). He's jealous because apparently the Queen* is not only allowed but is *expected* to prank-spell. *What*, I asked Puck, *is a PRANK-SPELL?* And he said it's exactly what it sounds like and looked at me like I was an especially stupid **toadbrain**.

"You know, spells to make people at the party laugh. Silly stuff like, last Halloween, the King magicked all the Seniors so they could only *hop* and their frogs so they could only *walk* and the year before that the Queen spell-swapped the teachers' clothes." Then he couldn't explain any more because he was laughing so hard at the memory of Mr Muddy wearing Ms Sparks's dress, but I think I get it.

* Or KING obvs.

2:49pm

In the end, the poem I read out in English was very short.

Light of the moon...
Behind the cloud
You seem very far away.

I pretended that it was so short because it was a haiku (?????), but it was really because I got so stressed reading the first verse aloud with everyone watching me that I had to ask Madam Binx if I could go to the toilet instead of reading the rest out.

8:15pm Home

I have a *cunning plan* ... which is why I've spent the last hour sitting on the floor of my bedroom, working on my husky voice and coughing skills, instead of doing my homework and recording the phases of the moon. A week or two at home, hiding and stealth-practising spelling and worrying about fractions, is the way to go.

In fact, it would probably be better for everyone if I became a HERMIT.

9:02pm

Dad heard me 'coughing' and came up to make me drink some medicine that was *almost* as disgusting as witch sausages because it would be "such a shame" if I was to miss school.

9:13pm

I do actually feel quite ill now.

TUESDAY 28TH SEPTEMBER

6:03pm Home

I forgot to take my diary with me to school today and I missed it *all day long*. I REFUSE to accept that Dad's got a point when he's says it's become my "comfort blanket". Ugh.

I talked to Stan A LOT, but he didn't talk back.

Winnie asked me if I was coming to lunch, but I said I had a packed lunch. She said I should still come and sit in the dining room with everyone else and that I couldn't "hide away somewhere scribbling in *that diary* forever". I one hundred per cent was going to do that but, when I got to the queue, Hunter and Blair and Izzi were in front of me, talking very loudly about how all the teachers were letting me get away with being

USELESS and why had I even been allowed to come to Extraordinary? So I decided that, after all, hiding in cupboards and ~~diarrizzing~~ scribbling is *lovely*.

The thing is, Hunter and Blair and Izzi are right. I'm not like them and even a **toadbrain** knows that at school not being like everyone else is very much NOT a good thing. And it's worse at this school because I'm *never* going to be like everyone else because **I CAN'T DO MAGIC.** *Obviously.*[*]

I miss my old school. I especially miss my old friends.

Dad's late home and, even if I can't talk to him about anything, I wish he'd hurry up and just *be* here.

6:50pm

Dad has just got home. He's bought a spacehopper. WHY?

6:57pm

Now he's bouncing round the garden. Who in their right mind *spacehops*????

---

[*] OK, I can manage to (mostly) stay on an ENCHANTED broom, but Blair's probably right when she says even a toadbrain could do that.

7:07pm

I take it all back: spacehopping is my new favourite thing.

WEDNESDAY 29TH SEPTEMBER

11:10am School

It's been a VERY stressful morning. I was late because halfway to school I realized I'd forgotten my wand and I had to run home at broom-speed to get it. Found it! *Phew!* (Dad had tidied it into the cutlery drawer beside the big spoons and the 'other' chopsticks.) That meant I was late picking up Stan and he was the only class frog left in the frog cubbyholes in reception. He looked quite pleased to be rescued from Mrs Slater. I don't think she likes frogs much more than she likes children.

In the end, I was twenty minutes late, but Miss Lupo was in a good mood and just told me to sit down and stop sweating and that I'd have to catch up.

She was scrawling another of her strange recipes on the whiteboard.

Ingredients

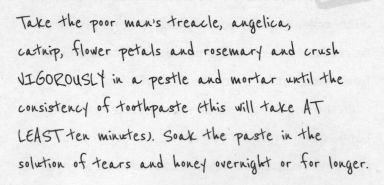

- 1 sprig rosemary · · · · ·
- 1 smashed clove poor man's treacle
- 1 tsp angelica
- 1 small bunch catnip
- 7 medium-sized cuckoo flower petals (fresh or dried)
- 1 vial tears of a baboon (if baboon tears are unavailable, substitute human tears)
- 1 tbsp runny honey
- 1 biscuit (any variety) · · · · ·

Take the poor man's treacle, angelica, catnip, flower petals and rosemary and crush VIGOROUSLY in a pestle and mortar until the consistency of toothpaste (this will take AT LEAST ten minutes). Soak the paste in the solution of tears and honey overnight or for longer.

"Right! You'll find angelica, catnip and rosemary in the school gardens and all you have to do is prepare the potion in your own time and bring it into class on the first Tuesday after the full Frost Moon – always such a good day for concoctions! Simple! So easy that even you lot can't mess it up!" I swear she was looking at me when she said that.

Puck, who'd somehow managed to turn his hair purple during the class, asked what the biscuit was for, and Miss Lupo said it was just in case we got hungry after all the VIGOROUS CRUSHING and that, if anyone preferred cake, she was absolutely fine with that. Then she **WHOOSHED** us all out of the classroom because her Year Ten class was waiting.

Wow, doesn't matter what school you go to, YEAR TEN are always scary.

I didn't get a chance to find out what the potion was *for*...

11:15am

I think I misjudged Blair!

She's just come to find me. At first, I thought it was so she could laugh at me for hiding in the first-floor cloak cupboard with Stan. To be fair, she did laugh at me, but then she showed me where the light switch was and explained she'd come to give me a copy of her notes from the Potions class because I'd missed lots of important stuff! She was only helping me "just this once", she said because she'd been in trouble with Lupo often enough to know it was no fun and they could all see I was *struggling* (which was hard to deny from the back of the cupboard, especially as Stan was nodding so hard, I thought his little froggy head was going to fall off).

I said thank you lots of times, and I was about to screw up my courage and ask her to show me how to loop-the-loop before the next **GO** match, when she announced she had better things to do than hang about with New Girls in cupboards and disappeared.

Anyway, once I'd got over how neat her handwriting was, I could see I really had missed *loads*. The second page was just the stuff I'd copied down off the board, but the whole of the first page was new to me.

Oh, and apparently it's a potion to get rid of SPOTS – finally something useful!

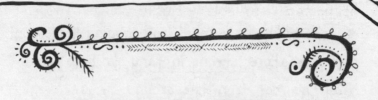

POTIONS NOTES

The most potent ingredient in this potion is the fingerlength of skeledrake root, which will be added, under supervision, to the other prepared ingredients in class. Bulbs grow thirteen centimetres deep under the knotted roots of the great wych elm in Nightshade Glade and MUST be extracted following these instructions:

* Leave your house not earlier than eleven o'clock, nor later than quarter past on the night of the full Frost Moon.
* Take with you a small iron digging implement and a creature, <u>strong in fang</u>, to help you drag the root from the ground.
* POLITELY direct your broomstick to take you to Nightshade Glade, taking the as-the-crow-flies route.
* When you reach Nightshade Glade, first honour the spirit of the Frost Moon by singing an original song and then the spirits of the forest by performing an original dance.
* On the <u>stroke of midnight</u>, dig for the roots and, when you have found them, call upon your creature to drag them from their hiding place.

11:35am

I've read the instructions three times now and it's all very INTENSE. I'd just been planning on nipping into the **Sensible Store** and adding some poor man's treacle and cuckoo flowers to the weekly shopping list. Actually, that's a lie. I've no idea what I was planning, but definitely not *this*. And Nightshade Glade is far deeper into the forest than I've ever gone. I'm not sure I'd be brave enough to go that far in the middle of the day, far less at MIDNIGHT, but if everyone else is there getting their roots too ... *maybe* it'll be fun?

Oh well, it's not due for ages. I'm going to forget all about it for now.

11:43am

An *original song*... Does that mean I have to *make one up*?

Dum-dee-dum-dee. Will there have to be words too? I can't imagine the Frost Moon enjoying this very much.

11:54am

I wonder what sort of dance it has to be? I'm not

really a dancing-in-moonlit-glades kind of girl.

Best to FORGET ABOUT IT for now.

12:15pm

Where am I going to get a 'creature strong in fang'?

Would a puppy count?

TO-DO LIST: V. URGENT

- Ask Dad for the millionth-zillionth time if I can
  PLEASE have a puppy.
- Remind Dad for the millionth-zillionth time to get
  me transferred to the **Academy** ASAP.

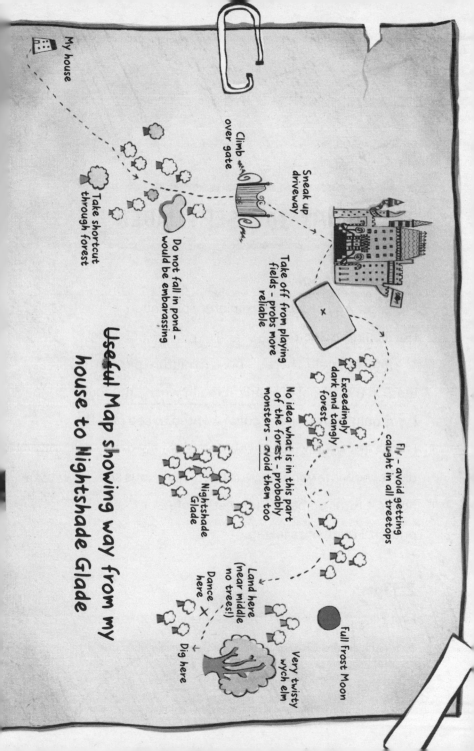

Useful Map showing way from my house to Nightshade Glade

My house

Take shortcut through forest

Climb over gate

Sneak up driveway

Do not fall in pond – would be embarrassing

Take off from playing fields – probs more reliable

Fly – avoid getting caught in all treetops

Exceedingly dark and tangly forest

No idea what is in this part of the forest – probably monsters – *avoid them too*

Nightshade Glade

Land here (near middle no trees!)

Dance here X

Dig here

Very twisty wych elm

Full Frost Moon

THURSDAY 30TH SEPTEMBER

10:52am School

Professor Agu brought a miniature pig called
Excalibur into Zoology!

Unfortunately, there's now a miniature pig on the
loose in the school grounds. It really wasn't my fault.
I was only joking when I said I wanted to see pigs fly.
I didn't know Puck would take me seriously and I
didn't know the window was open. Blair says she
hopes it turns up before it meets Professor Crisp's
python. I *think* she's joking.

2:43pm

First History class with Professor Crisp who is even
older than Mrs Slater. In fact, he is so EXTREMELY

old, I suspect he's lived through most of what he's teaching us. He didn't seem to have a python with him... I hope it hasn't gone on a pig hunt.

I can't concentrate for worrying about Excalibur.

History homework:

Write a 300-word essay on witchcraft during the Roman period, with particular reference to witch gladiators. Extra marks will be given for illustrations.

11:59pm Home

Too worried about Excalibur to sleep.

FRIDAY 1ST OCTOBER

9:03am School

Met the Year Eight class frog on the way to registration and I have FROG ENVY. It's a neon-green tree frog called Pablo and he's the cutest, most upbeat ~~amfibbeean~~ hoppy-thing I've ever seen.

I feel *so bad* for Stan.

10:56am

Just got out of PE and, even though I had to give Fabi back his lucky sock after he fell off his broom three times in five minutes, I *still* scored FIVE goals!!!!!

Even Blair, captain of the Dragons, congratulated me. "Well done, Bea! What a FLUKE! So sorry about the injury." Now I know her better, I'm sure she hadn't meant to crash me into the turret – it was a rough game.

Final score:

DODOS: 43   DRAGONS: 42

One hundred per cent worth the concussion.

6:13pm Home

I've got a bump the size of an EGG on my forehead. Dad's got a bump on his head too because he got caught in a mini-storm of hailstones the size of ONIONS as he was spacehopping home after a happy day studying lightning scorch marks on the UnCommon, so we're both sitting here with packets of frozen peas on our foreheads and I'm trying to dodge his questions about my homework.

"Just a bit of Chemistry," I say vaguely. My peas were getting warm with the effort not to tell him EVERYTHING. I'd tried to distract him by mentioning that I'd spotted a triple rainbow over the school bell tower.

He got very excited – apparently, it's incredibly rare but not *impossible* (unlike some of the things I've seen at Extraordinary). Then I told him I really NEEDED a puppy ASAP, one with teeth, and he blinked and looked a bit sad and said *he* was always here for me to talk to if I was lonely.

11:32pm

Couldn't sleep so I stayed up making a tiny yellow Dodo bib for Stan to wear at the next **GO** match out of an old pair of knickers. Pretty sure Year Eight Pablo doesn't have one of those.

The Extraordinary: Halloween Term Issue 1

Sports News and Notices

- Congratulations to the Year Ten Shooting Stars who <u>crushed</u> the Year Eleven Flying Cauldrons by 231 goals to 165.

- Ms Celery would like to remind all GOers that head-on broom-bumping is an ILLEGAL MOVE that (if seen) will be penalized. We all wish Gerty Twistle a speedy recovery.

Halloween Ball Notices

- Year Seven and Eight: applications to join the Junior Halloween Ball Committee (with particular responsibility for menu choices and decoration) must be made to Ms Sparks <u>no later than 4:30pm Friday</u>.

- Year Nine, Ten and Eleven: those who wish to join the teachers on the Senior Halloween Ball Committee are very welcome. Planning meetings will be Wednesday and Friday after school in the Little Library. Just turn up with your BEST ideas!

Quick-fire Q & A with Ms Sparks!

Q: *Favourite time of the year?*

A: Halloween of course!

Q: *Favourite pet?*

A: *Long pause while head thinks* ~~Um, I had a dog when I was little, a cockerpoo called Bubble~~ ZEPHYR OF COURSE!

Q: *Favourite joke?*

A: What goes cackle, cackle, bonk? A witch laughing her head off!

Thank you, Ms Sparks!

Dear Agony Witch

Dear Agony Witch,

X in my class is a twin. Y in my class is also a twin. X and Y keep swapping places and then laughing at me when I call them by the wrong name. While the rest of the class find this very funny, I feel it is undermining my authority. I cannot tell which witch is which, what should I do?

Yours,

A Worried Teacher

Dear Worried Teacher,

I suggest you turn one into a warthog, easily distinguished from a witch. Problem solved. Have a great term.

Love,

Agony Witch x

WEDNESDAY 6TH OCTOBER

3:45pm School

Just got out of Physics and Mr Muddy said my attempt at levitating Stan "demonstrated real progress". What I didn't tell him was that that was *at least* ninety-nine per cent* down to Stan's helpful leap at the big moment. "You'll be flying that frog across the classroom in no time," he said.

Maybe not.

* One hundred per cent!

THURSDAY 7TH OCTOBER

10:55am School

BEST news. Ms Celery flew into the middle of our Zoology class, looking hot and bothered and very cross. Well, that wasn't the best news – the *best* news was that Excalibur has turned up alive and well in her gym bag.

I'm not a miniature-pig murderer!

I'm lucky she found him because that bag is SO big and SO full of peculiar things that he could have been in there for days with nothing to eat but energy bars and nothing to drink but get-better potions.

Professor Agu was so happy he forgot all about testing us on the magical properties of ducks and let us out early for break.

Ms Celery's gym bag contents:

2 packets of
Sir Scary Cook's
energy bars

Concise Guide to
Cheating at GO (vol. 3)

1 bottle of 'Get
Back on the Pitch'
potion

1 pair of cat-shaped
dumbells

1 miniature pig

FRIDAY 8TH OCTOBER
(FROST MOON EVE! EEEEEEK!!!)

11:01am School

| DODOS: 52 | DRAGONS: 40 |

Ms Celery asked me after PE if I'd like to be vice-captain of the Dodos after half-term! I was so excited I forgot to tell her I'd probably have moved schools by then

12:15pm

It is a shame that PE is followed by Maths.

Mr Smith kept me back after class for a Little Chat. "Have you any idea what could happen if you get the maths in a potion wrong?" he asked quite kindly before embarking on a terrifying story about a student who

117

magicked a mouse
the size of a rhino
(some mistakes are
harder to hide than
others). "You can crack
this, Bea Black," he said as I
was finally escaping. "And, if you get stuck again, just
come and ask me and I'll help you."

I like Mr Smith now. Still don't like fractions though.

2:47pm

Very useful Friday lecture
about trees. I'm now ~~a bit~~
confident that I will be
able to recognize a ~~WITCH~~
WYCH ELM.

Then the Year Elevens
did an aerial acrobatics
display that as far as I could
work out had absolutely nothing
to do with trees, but it was so *amaaaazzzzinggg*

I clapped until my hands hurt. (Maybe if I was invisible, and *nobody ever asked me to do MAGIC,*[*] this school would be OK???)

3:35pm

Things are looking up on the Potions front! Amara asked me if I wanted her spare cuckoo flowers, but before I could thank her, far less ask if she had any helpful tips on skeledrakes, she shoved a brown paper bag of the flowers into my hand and flew off. Oh well, I guess I'll see her in the forest tomorrow night and can thank her then.

5:21pm Home

Mrs Slater had seemed surprised when, instead of checking Stan into his cubbyhole at going-home time, I asked to keep him for the weekend. At first, I thought she was going to say no, but it was just her very-angry-tortoise face.

"What do you want with *him*?" she asked, looking

[*] *Or original song-and-dance routines.*

at Stan as though he was a very disappointing frog. Excuse me! Stan is, in his own way, a FAB frog. But that wasn't why I was taking him on a little holiday to No. 1 Piggoty Lane. I still need a creature strong in fang and, even if Stan's teeth are tiny, any toothed creature has to be better than none. Probably.

"You can dig up a skeledrake root – whatever that is – can't you?" I'd asked him while we were walking home (well, I was walking; Stan was in my cape pocket). He hadn't given me what you could call a direct answer but, when I peeked at him, he didn't look any more downbeat than usual so I was taking that as a YES.

5:52pm

"You don't happen to know what poor man's treacle is, do you?" I asked Dad, on the off-chance.

"Garlic," he replied without missing a beat. "Haven't heard it called that in a long time." My dad is literally a GENIUS. "Why do you want to know?"

120

"School quiz on old plant names," I ~~lied~~ said, and he nodded happily, like that made perfect sense. He doesn't seem to mind that there's a frog on the kitchen table – completely bought my garbled ~~second lie~~ explanation about Observing Wild Creatures Up Close for Zoology. In fact, he was so impressed by the enlightened teaching methods *blah blah* at Extraordinary that it might have hurt my Move School Campaign.

Tragically, he's never heard of baboon tears so I think I'll just substitute my own and hope for the best. I've ticked off *nearly* everything on page two of my Potions homework!

Honestly, if it wasn't for the whole ~~skeledrakes-midnight-digging~~ thing, I'd be chill about this homework.

6:33pm
I've discovered Stan likes ~~burnt~~ crispy fish fingers! I'm not sure that's OK. It's practically CANNIBALISM. For a small frog he has a big appetite.

8:13pm

Ash came over – he's just left.

"Is that a FROG on your head?" he asked the minute he came through the door.

"Of course," I said, nodding (*carefully*). Then I remembered this wasn't NORMAL and blabbered out my Zoology excuse. Ash looked confused. Apparently, the only frogs that turn up in lessons at the **Academy** have been dead for some time. He started to tell me about a 'fun' dissection class, but it was too scary for Stan* so I had to make him stop. Then he asked me if I wanted to go round to his tomorrow – some of his friends from school were coming over to watch football and eat pizza. For about two seconds, I was really happy and then I remembered...

Nooooo!

My first invitation to a sort-of-party in Little Spellshire and I can't go because I'll be too BUSY preparing to FLY off into the forest to DIG and perform a midnight SONG-AND-DANCE routine.

I am NOT really happy any more.

---

* Look, I can't be SURE he understands, but I can't be sure he doesn't????

I said I'd be finishing my homework and Ash looked at me like I was a tragic *worm* and went home in a huff.

9:13pm

Turns out a) crying to order is very hard (even after my big disappointment about missing out on pizza and football) and b) collecting tears in an old shampoo bottle is even harder. I might just use water with a bit of salt – it's all the same, isn't it?

9:32pm

Dad heard me 'crying' and came up to ask me if I had *friend problems.*

I said NO quite aggressively because of not having very many friends at all and then we (Stan too) sat on the edge of my bed in silence for five minutes.

"Well, something's wrong," Dad said at last.

"How did you know?" I asked, which was very STUPID and he said that even if I hadn't been "howling like a sad dog" it was "written all over my face".

For a minute, I let myself imagine what it would be like to tell Dad what was going on because, even though he probably wouldn't have any tips on digging up skeledrakes, he'd make me feel better. Instead, I asked him if he'd managed to find out if I could transfer schools and he said that he hadn't wanted to mention it earlier when I sounded so upbeat about my homework (!) but actually YES, the request has been lodged. Then he looked at me sadly, handed me a tissue and said it was likely for the best because he wasn't *convinced* I'd settled at Extraordinary.

So ... that's good news.

"Of course," he said, handing me the whole box of tissues, "there's no guarantee that the Academy will agree to take you."

Might manage to collect those tears after all.

10:13pm

Stan is sitting on my pillow like something out of a fairy tale. I hope he's not thinking about turning into a prince. I would not be OK with that.

SATURDAY 9TH OCTOBER

10:46pm Home

Nearly time to go to Nightshade Glade and I've got a bad case of THE DREADS.

Part of me is super up for some midnight-y, magic-y, moonlight-y mayhem but a bigger part of me is super FREAKING OUT. What did Dad say last night? Write a list of the things that are worrying you and you'll see they're not so bad… It's worth a go, I guess.

Things That Are ESPECIALLY Worrying Me RIGHT NOW

1. The risk of not getting off the ground. I ~~may~~ have messed up a bit on forward-planning

by bringing a frog home and not a broomstick because I can now confirm that ordinary kitchen brooms/ brushes/mops do not fly. Not even the Hoover. Nope. Zero enchantment + zero witch skills = zero levitation.[*] I know this because I tried them all (which was embarrassing when Dad spotted me in the garden astride a mop, snorted and asked if I was "still playing *pretend-horsey*" which was a) not funny and b) a bit much coming from the grown man who'd bought a spacehopper).

2. *If* I get off the ground, the risk that I'll get lost and/or stranded.

3. *If* lost and/or stranded in the forest, risk that I'll be eaten by a wolf. (Or other munchy creature hiding in the trees. A *werewolf*?? More interesting, but also probably more deadly.)

4. *If*, against the odds, I reach Nightshade Glade, the risk of messing up the spell/incantation/

[*] *Practically Maths.*

magic dance/digging part of the evening.

This risk is very high. Possibly also deadly.

Yep, still freaking out. *Anyhoooo*, nearly time to go.

10:55pm

Have panic-eaten half a packet of custard creams.
Feel a bit sick.

OK, I don't have time to waste sitting around
eating. I don't even have time to sit around
panicking and I definitely don't have time to
be writing this diary.

10:59pm

Finished the custard creams. Must just triple-check
my checklist.

☑ **1 torch**
☑ **1 spade**

☑ 1 bag for life (to put freshly dug-up skeledrake root in)

☑ ~~Many biscuits~~ (eaten)

☑ 1 ~~creature strong in fang~~ frog

☐ 1 broomstick

All that's left is to stop at the school on my way and borrow a broomstick. Simple.

11:00pm

Is it simple though?

I really need to go!

SUNDAY 10TH OCTOBER

1:32am Home

On the upside, I'm back in my bedroom.

On the downside, I don't have any skeledrake root.

On the double-downside, I think that might be the least of my worries...

At first, everything seemed to be going to plan. The school looked even more like a haunted castle than usual in the moonlight. I pushed the door open ... and nearly fell over with shock. Staring back at me in the dark was row upon row of tiny, glittery eyes! **Croak, ribbit, croak.** Thankfully, it was only the left-behind class frogs watching me from their night-time cubbyholes and hailing their adventurous fellow frog, Stan-the-Man. There was no sign of Mrs Slater.

All good.

I slip-slid across the marble floor to the broom cupboard and two minutes later I was back outside, trying to find room on the broomstick for a spade, a torch, a bag for life, a frog and me.

"Nightshade Glade, please," I asked my broom as if it was a friendly bus conductor, and with a grumpy lurch it was off. Within seconds, I was over the twisty chimneys. WHOOOOSH! A sharp left and I was over the treetops.

TRAGICALLY, it turns out that flying over – and then, when the broom dropped down, *through* – a forest when you're not sure where you're going, the batteries in your torch have run out and the moon keeps going behind clouds, is nothing like flying over the sports pitch. I had several nasty run-ins with branches that seemed to come out of nowhere, a trio of owls and something unidentifiable but very spiky. *Anyway*, I'm not entirely sure how I got there, but I finally landed in the glade. The moon had come out again and I could see that someone – probably Miss

Lupo – had recently Sellotaped a big sign to the trunk of the twistiest wych elm: Get Your Skeledrakes Here!

B-but ... *where was everyone?*

Where was *anyone?* I must have made up more time on the broom than I'd thought, but it was a bit odd that I hadn't seen a single witch on the way here. Still, I wasn't going to hang around waiting for them. I was a relatively small and extremely USELESS witch person and I seriously wanted to get out of this forest (*what even were those howling sounds?*) but, more to the point, I'd have been mad to wait for an audience for my original song-and-dance routine!

With a heartfelt apology to the Frost Moon, I filled my lungs and warbled:

"Oh, Frost Moon,
Oh, Moon of Frost,
You gleam so bright,
I cannot get lost."

I couldn't really blame it for going behind a cloud at that exact moment. Taking advantage of the darkness, I threw in some ~~classy~~ dance moves, twirling and bowing in the direction of the tangliest bushes to honour the forest spirits.

"Oh, Frost Moon,
You shine above,
Tralalala,
The Goddess of Love,"

I trilled mid-pirouette and Stan added a couple of **ribbbitts** to the mix.

"Tralalalala...
Lalala..."

I couldn't remember the next line (probably for the best) so I really went for it with some original shimmying – all those hours watching *Strictly* with Dad were really paying off! Stan was doing his very best to partner me, hopping around like his little froggy life depended on it. This was more fun than I thought it would be.

It was the noise that made me look up.

Aaaaarrgh! Stan leaped on to my shoulder and we both looked heavenwards and PANICKED. What was *that?*

Skimming over the treetops was not a grateful lunar spirit but a fizzing, spitting FIREBALL.

Wait ... TWO fireballs ... no ... one of them was a CAT and the other ... was my HEADMISTRESS!

"*What. Do. You. Think. You. Are. Doing?*"

"Er—" There was a *looonnnng*, painful pause. "D-d-dancing?"

Ms Sparks landed and said she could see that and for a second I thought she was going to laugh. But no. *Nooooo.* She was very, very cross. So cross that she wasn't just sparks by name: there was a halo of angry, fiery specks all round her head!

"WHAT. ARE. YOU. DOING. IN. THE. MIDDLE. OF.
THE. NIGHT. IN. THE. FOREST?"

I tried to explain that I was digging up skeledrake
roots, but she seemed to
think this was a very poor
explanation. "*WHAT
ARE SKELEDRAKES?*"
Why was she asking
me? She was going to
set fire to a tree if she
didn't calm down. I tried
to ignore the fact that a
sheepish frog was now doing
his best to hide down the back of my shirt collar
– *eeeurgh* – and blurted out that I was just collecting
ingredients for my Potions homework. It might have
been the truth, but it didn't impress her. It really was
bad luck that she'd turned up *and* nobody else had.

"But how did you—" I began, but she didn't let me
answer before she told me if I was going to the forest
to BREAK SCHOOL RULES (*ooops*) it was a TERRIBLE

idea to stop off at school on the way.

"But it was in her notes—" I began and Ms Sparks stopped asking WHY and started asking WHAT NOTES? And WHOSE NOTES? *Tricky.*

"Hand them over," she demanded, fixing me with such a Steely Glare I looked away and caught Zephyr's eye instead (big mistake: that cat was terrifying). I stood there, my mouth opening and closing like a goldfish. I might be in DEEP trouble, but something told me that handing over these notes wasn't going to make anything any easier.

"Great giggling GOATS," began Ms Sparks.

What now? My pocket was twitching like it was home to a ferret...

"Give me those NOTES!"

Out flew the notes and I watched, cringing, as they turned a show-offy somersault in the air and landed neatly in the open mouth of the little gold handbag propped on the end of the headmistress's broom. "Right," she said as the handbag snapped itself shut with a superior *tut*, "I'll see you in my office Monday morning at nine o'clock. Sharp."

And that was that. With a single wave of her wand, I was back on my borrowed broom and, in what felt like an instant, back here in my bedroom, writing this down because there is no way I'm getting to sleep. Too much to worry about.

Will I get a detention?

Will I get suspended?

Will I get expelled? Ex*SPELLED*?

Not sure how I feel about that.

1:52am

I keep thinking about Blair's notes. Did she make a mistake? There must be an explanation.

2:33am

There IS a possible explanation, but it's not very nice...

2:55am

Could it really have been a joke??? Right now, it doesn't feel very funny.

8:59pm

Today has been a very BAD day.

And *no*, Dad's persistent attempts to find out what was wrong with me and then cheer me up by a) saying every five minutes, "Whatever it is, it can't be *that* bad!" (wrong) and b) feeding me burnt cheese toasties didn't help.

Not even FLUFFMALLOWS helped.

8:58am School

So here I am, back outside the headmistress's office ...
in for it. Again.

Blair's inside right now and, even though I can't
hear exactly what Ms Sparks is saying, I can tell she's
NOT happy. I shouldn't think Blair's very happy either,
but she doesn't seem to be getting a word in.

She was already waiting when I arrived and I was
just winding myself up to ask her WHY she'd sent
me off into the deep, dark forest in the middle of the
night on my own* to dig up skeledrakes (what even
were they?) when she greeted me with, "Witches that
snitches end up in ditches," and catapulted a **GO** ball
straight over my head and into a large nearby urn

---

* Except for a frog.

full of daisies and a family of visiting toads.

The good news was that none of the toads (which are still hopping crossly around my ankles) were harmed, but the bad news was that now I felt a) guilty and b) a bit worried that that was an actual SPELL. So I told her that I hadn't snitched to Ms Sparks and I hadn't *meant* to hand over the notes. It had just *happened*.

I don't know if she believed me because all she said was, "I wish I'd seen your original dance."

Er ... *was she trying not to laugh*?

"Did the Frost Moon LOVE it?" She was definitely laughing! And then Stan (who was meant to be here for moral support) started shaking in exactly the way I'd expect a frog to shake if a frog could get a fit of the giggles. Traitor!

"What about the song?" Blair snorted. "Did the tree spirits join in?"

Were the TOADS laughing at me now too? This was the opposite of funny *except* ... there's something very catching about giggles when you're in trouble.

"You could just have got me back," she said but, before I could stop sniggering and ask her for any helpful tips on revenge, Zephyr put her head round the door, followed a second later by Ms Sparks and no one was laughing any more.

9:11am

Blair's just come out – nope, definitely not laughing now.

"Your turn," she says, glaring at me. "Have fun."

GULP.

9:31am

Well, that was odd.

Ms Sparks didn't give me biscuits this time. Instead, she gave me a very long and painful LECTURE. So now I know:

1. Skeledrake root is not a thing. Apparently, even a **toadbrain** would know that (she didn't put it quite like that).

2. It would be most unusual for a Year Seven potion to need ingredients that could not be found a) in the school gardens, b) on the shelves of the lab or c) in Mr Riggle's Emporium on the High Street.

3. The forest was very dangerous at night and not a place to be "prancing around" on my own. I asked her what the howling noises were and she said that it wasn't a good time to "PANIC me any further".

4. For future reference, frogs are NOT creatures strong in fang.* Zephyr seemed to find that particular misunderstanding very funny.

5. Ms Sparks didn't say anything about Blair's notes, but she did suggest that it was good to keep an open mind, but not so open that my brains fell out.

Then she asked me, in a much kinder voice, whether I was finally getting the hang of levitation. I said "sort of" which was a lie. She seemed pleased

* It didn't seem like the right moment to ask her about puppies.

because apparently levitation was an early witch skill to "come in" and, once I had that under my belt, the sky was the limit. Haha.

It was my punishment that was the really ODD bit. I haven't been expelled or suspended or even got a detention. Instead, I've been ordered to join the *Junior Halloween Ball Committee*. This makes NO sense. PARTY PLANNING? I mean, I like parties (or at least I used to before I became someone whose favourite place to hang out was a broom cupboard and whose best friend was a frog). It doesn't sound *that* bad ... but then nothing at this school ever turns out to be the way it sounds.

9:45am

Apparently, Blair's punishment is to clean out all the frog cubicles without using magic for the rest of the term. She's still not laughing. I don't think she's talking to me any more either. Amara says she's really lucky to still be Queen of Mischief and that Ms

Sparks must have forgotten about it. I don't think Blair is feeling 'really lucky' – she doesn't seem to be a big frog fan. I don't think she'll ever show me how to do loop-the-loops now.

1:11pm

A very neat and detailed, colour-coded and highlighted schedule was sitting on my desk after lunch. The Post-it note stuck to the front read:

I was already panicking when Hunter walked past, looked over my shoulder and drawled, "I wouldn't go on THAT committee if you paid me – not with *her* in charge. She's a tyrant, like literally the bossiest witch in the school." He shuddered theatrically. "Good luck."

On second thoughts, I wouldn't mind cleaning out the frog cubbyholes with Blair.

7:02pm Home

I accidentally told Dad I'd joined the Halloween Ball planning committee and now he thinks I'm super KEEN and *finally* making an effort to try to settle into my new school. He looks so pleased and relieved I don't have the heart to tell him it's *not quite like that*.

He's now halfway through a very embarrassing story about him falling into a cake at a party when he was my age. Sometimes I worry.

"Your costume is going to be AMAZING by the way," he says.

Moving school, preferably before HALLOWEEN, is now CRITICAL.

8:45pm

I'm sitting in bed, having a practice, one-person brainstorming session. I want to make the right impression at tomorrow's committee meeting so they don't think I'm the most useless **toadbrain** of all useless **toadbrains**. Also, I'm frightened of the TYRANT-IN-CHARGE.

Right. I need a proper list like a proper, organized, brain-stormy sort of ~~witch~~ person.

FOOD

(NOT made by Sir Scary Cook and as non-witchy as possible)

- Lots of crisp-like things (esp. Pringles)
- Biscuits (must inc. Oreos)
- Cakes (do I have time to learn to BAKE????)
- Something special for the frogs to eat??? (NOT fish fingers)

PARTY MUST-HAVES

- Playlist
- Disco ball????

145

HALLOWEEN VIBES

- Fake candles
- Pumpkin-carving station?
- Apple bobbing
- Station for fake, Halloweeny make-up!
- Fake bats/bat bunting??
- Fake skeletons
- Fake spiders' webs

It is an EPIC list, so fingers crossed the committee president doesn't eat me alive (although that would be quite Halloweeny).

Zoology homework:
Read Chapter 4 of Ambius Ambrose's Animalium Magicum.

TUESDAY 12ᵀᴴ OCTOBER

1:55pm School

OK, so I've just come out of the meeting and it was
NOT what I was expecting.

The scary-TYRANT-committee-
chair was only Winnie ~~Boss~~
Ross! It's true that she had
three clipboards, one of those
little hammer things judges
have and a MEGAPHONE (which
she was not afraid to use), but she's
always been nice to me. Amara and Puck and Fabi
are all on the committee as well – I didn't ask if they'd
been forced to sign up too.

Winnie was pleased I'd made a list (she *really*

likes lists) and she lent me a clipboard *and the megaphone* so I could read it out to the whole committee. But ... it turns out witches do Halloween and parties *slighhhhtllyyyyy* differently. First of all, I offended everyone with my list of shop-bought food.

"Why would we eat that?" Amara seemed genuinely confused. "Sir Cook makes the best party cakes in the world."

I remembered the sausages and shuddered.

Puck lobbed a mini cupcake at me.

OK, it looked delicious, it even smelled good, but I wasn't going to make the same mistake twice. No witch food was ever going to cross my lips again. I palmed it off on Stan as discreetly as I could and moved on.

By the time I got to the end of my list, everyone was laughing, literally rolling around on the floor, snorting and sniggering.

"First off," Winnie said after she'd finally stopped laughing and taken back her megaphone, "you can cross out all the *fakes*."

I was confused and said that obviously we couldn't have *real* skeletons?!

That went down very badly. Apparently, it's Indiana's favourite night of the whole year. Who is Indiana you might ask? I certainly did. Well, it's INDIANA BONES – the live skeleton (well, *probably* not actually *live*, but you know what I mean) who lives in the senior science lab.

"And why would we need FAKE Halloween make-up?" asked Amara, rolling her eyes. "Demo time." She wiggled her wand, said a little chant and just like that her skin turned bright orange.

Apple bobbing was another no-no – teen witches in costume, explained Puck, shaking his long hair like a wet dog, were not overly keen on sticking their heads in buckets.

"*Wait...*" Winnie, who'd grabbed my list and was crossing things out furiously, paused, pen in hand, "the bat bunting's not a TERRIBLE idea."

I started to feel smug, but then a witch from Year

Eight called Fred said it was a BASIC and ORDINARY idea and everyone except me nodded.

"True," said Winnie, "but real bats are a NIGHTMARE at parties."

More enthusiastic nodding and I joined in this time because, even though I'd never met a real bat at a party, I couldn't *imagine* they were great guests.

"They can get a bit *hyper*," admitted Puck who was hanging upside down from the curtain pole at the time.

"Yeah, they always drink too much and get hysterical," added Fabi.

"So? How does it work?" Amara (who was now only thirty per cent tangerine) asked me. "We spell some bunting?"

"Noooooo!" I said. "We MAKE it. It's not hard." I crossed my fingers. I might not know *exactly* how to make bat bunting, but I had no idea how to SPELL it.* "It'll be fun."

They all looked at me like I'd suggested cleaning

* Or anything else.

out the frogs, but then Winnie said that it was important to be open to new ways of doing things, however *backward*, and that anyway I needed something to be busy with that wasn't too *demanding*. I would have been offended except that a) she was totally right and b) she high-fived me when she said it.

So my official job – announced by megaphone and recorded in the meeting minutes – is now **Witch In Charge Of Bat Bunting**.

7:01pm Home

Dad's been home for ages, but it looks like I'm making tea. He has locked himself in the garden shed and won't let me in. "It will spoil the surprise!" he shouted through the door.

I've had too many surprises in the last few weeks. I HATE surprises now.

7:33pm

Toast for tea it is. I've got a lot to do.

HOW TO MAKE BAT BUNTING

- Find a picture of a bat and then copy its shape on to a piece of card or paper. This might take a few goes (don't give up if early attempts look like pigeons or manta rays or tents).
- OR ... you could trace over this helpful bat template right here...
- Halloween bats are traditionally black but, if orange or purple bats are your thing, go for it. Feel free to stick big, googly eyes on your bats too. Added glitter or neon stripes can also add to the Halloween vibe.
- Make LOADS of bats and then carefully hole-punch the edges of each bat's wings and string them all together with thick black thread or cord.

8:45pm

Operation Bat Bunting is underway!

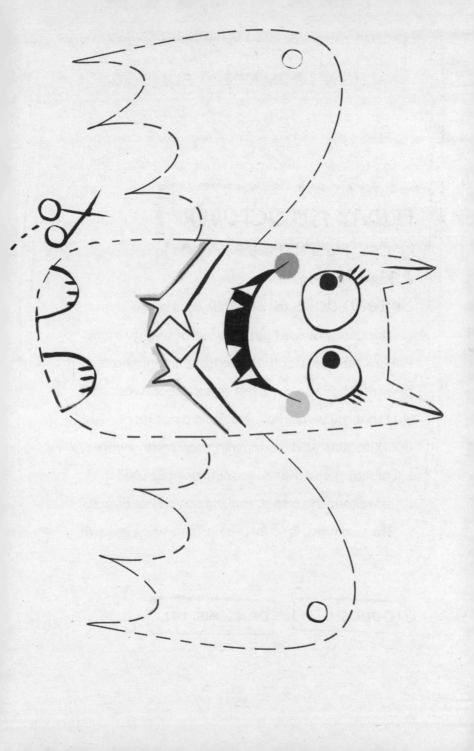

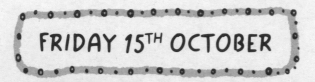

FRIDAY 15TH OCTOBER

8:33pm Home

Sixteen days to Halloween. Very busy.

The good news is I got nine out of twenty in my Potions test. OK, not *that* good, but it could have been much worse. Puck got three out of twenty. It's true that my very smelly potion did not work AT ALL, but Miss Lupo said my crushing and mixing were satisfactory *and* that it was surprisingly TASTY. At least it wasn't a spot-*making* potion like Puck's.

The bad news is so BAD it hurts to write it down. Today's GO score...

DODOS: 0   DRAGONS: 141

I don't know if it makes it better or worse, but what I *and everyone else wearing a yellow Dodo bib* say is that balls don't just "jump back out" of the chimney EVERY SINGLE TIME without FOUL PLAY. Ms Celery says she didn't see anything (????) and if we suspected cheating then we should "get off our butts and use our wands". I'm not sure what she meant by that, but I'm beginning to think that what gets you into trouble at witch school is not always the same as at ordinary school.

The Dragons were VERY SMUG. Blair did an entire circuit of loop-the-loops to celebrate. She really is annoyingly good on a broomstick.

Bat Bunting Tally: thirty-seven (would have been more but it's hard to concentrate on cutting out bats after your team's been DESTROYED).

SATURDAY 16TH OCTOBER

4:43pm Taffy Tallywick's Teashop
Fifteen days till Halloween.

Winnie called an Emergency Saturday Committee Meeting, which is why I'm sitting in the teashop, with the kitten on my feet, taking the minutes.

1. Clean the **Great Hall**.
2. Clean and polish all 107 of the special silver **Halloween** cake stands and all 33 of the special golden punchbowls.

I just saw Ash and some of his friends walking past the window! I gave him a little awkward wave and

he gave a little awkward wave back and then one of the boys he was with said something to him and he went red. Amara asked me if he was the boy I'd tried to introduce her to in Rhubarb & Custard and, when I said he was, she gave a little awkward wave too, but Ash pretended he didn't see her and started walking faster.

"Does your friend go to the Academy?" asked Winnie.

"Yes, and he's really nice," I said quite firmly.

They all looked at each other until Winnie declared it was time to get back to business.

People in this town need to get a grip.

Anyway, where was I?

3. Ask Mr Zicasso for more black card and glue from the art-room supplies.
4. Arrange a small gold throne for Zephyr. *Seriously?*
5. Clean the Great Chandelier.

It's beginning to dawn on me that the Junior Committee's responsibilities involve A LOT of cleaning.

Bat Bunting Tally: fifty-nine (would have been sixty but Puck spilled hot chocolate on one).

SUNDAY 17TH OCTOBER

7:13pm Home

Went round to Ash's to see if I could borrow some glue. Neither of us mentioned **Taffy Tallywick's**, but when I asked if we could hang out at half-term he said, "Definitely!" His mum had just finished cutting his hair and his fringe is now so terrifyingly straight that he looks like a Lego figure. Anyway, I was glad I managed not to laugh because Mrs Namdar asked me to stay for tea and it was meatballs. Yum!

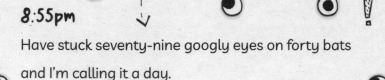

8:55pm

Have stuck seventy-nine googly eyes on forty bats
and I'm calling it a day.

Trying not to think about school tomorrow.
Obviously, I'm dreading another day of failing
TRAGICALLY at all things witchy, *but* there's only
fourteen days till Halloween. So much to do!
Must remember to get more GOOGLY EYES.

9:09pm

Thinking about school tomorrow. ~~Slightly~~ Regretting
not ~~finishing~~ starting my History homework.

---

*Make a model of a medieval witch castle including
potion laboratory, high walls for protection from
Ordinaries, magical moat, Great Banqueting Hall and
broomstick landing pad.*

MONDAY 18TH OCTOBER

9:01am School

Thirteen days till Halloween.

I asked Winnie how much bunting we'd need and she said at least twelve strings. I didn't think that sounded too bad until she added that each string should have at least A HUNDRED bats strung on it. I asked her if she was joking, but she asked me if I'd seen the size of the **Great Hall**.

1:55pm

The **Great Hall** looks even GREATER with all the chairs packed away. Winnie's right: we're going to need *a lot of bunting*. Also, dusting this place is going to take us until *next* Halloween. I thought Winnie would just wave her wand, but apparently we're only allowed to do tidying-up spells in class because Ms Sparks says, "All Extraordinary witches must also learn to be competent at ordinary life skills," and that, "Broom skills don't start and stop with flying." Disappointing!

I pointed out all the cobwebs we'd have to clear to Winnie, but she just looked at me like I was a terrible person. She said that we had to ask their owners nicely and then clean *under* the webs – SPIDERS deserved to live here as much as the rest of us.

I suppose it sort of makes sense???

According to Winnie's clipboard, one of the teachers is going to take down the Great Chandelier for us this week so we can polish it.

I'd forgotten just how BIG that chandelier was.

7:32pm Home

Bat Bunting Tally: 185. I've stepped up production. (I was hoping Dad would help, but he's locked himself in the shed again.)

THURSDAY 21ST OCTOBER

6:49pm Home

A LOT happened on Tuesday, which meant that this diary needed a couple of days off to lie quietly in my sock drawer and recover.

I'd had a feeling things were going too smoothly. I should have known when I passed my fractions test (fourteen out of twenty, *woo-hoo*, thank you, Mr Smith!) that my day had peaked. But Madam Binx lulled me into a false sense of security. Literally.

"This spell will help you be at one with your inner-calm-witch," she announced in her sing-song voice while watering her Venus flytrap. "It's one of my favourites."

I sighed so loudly everyone turned to look at me.

163

My inner-*anything*-witch had yet to show up.

"Mallowmoons," she murmured.

"Bibbblyblossommms. *Clllllooooouddsss*."

My eyes were drooping (although that could have been because I'd stayed up all night punching holes in cardboard bat wings).

"A serene witch is a powerful witch because they are not wasting their energy on frenetic nonsense— IS THERE ANY REASON, PUCK BERRY," she yelled, "FOR YOU TO BE PUTTING THAT BAT DOWN FABI'S CLOAK?"

"It's not a real bat!" Puck said (it was one of my cut-out bats). "Even I wouldn't be stupid enough to bring a REAL bat into class."

Madam Binx tried to look cross, but she had a soft spot for Puck. "You all have a lot of work to do on your inner calm," she said, rolling her eyes. "Right, sit quietly for two minutes and think soothing thoughts while I nip to Miss Lupo's room and borrow some lavender. That might help. I'm trusting you," she said and closed the door.

One minute Blair was sitting at her desk looking serene and the next minute, with a **WHOOSH**, she was standing beside me.

"Well, what do we have here? Bea's *diary*." And before I even knew what was happening, she was waving my diary – THIS DIARY – in the air. "*Ooooooh! Top secret*." She sniggered. "*Tuesday the twenty-first of September, one forty five. Woke up sweating. I'd had this* terrifying *nightmare that I'd gone to a school full of WITCHES and FROGS*," she read in a silly voice that I think was meant to sound like me.

I LAUNCHED myself at her and made a GRAB. Too late! She'd tossed my diary high in the air – up, up, up and *noooooooo!* down, down ... *into the open jaws of Binxy's Venus flytrap...*

SNAP!

Some witches were laughing, but not all of them. I didn't even care – I was too busy gulping back tears and trying to persuade a POT PLANT to give me back my diary.

It was Winnie who came to my rescue. "Spit it out!" she said very firmly to the flytrap. The big plant shook its spiky trap. "SPIT IT OUT AT ONCE! It's forgotten it's carnivorous. AT ONCE!"

And finally, because it was hard to say no to Winnie, with a huge BELCH, the flytrap burped back out my diary and I scrambled to pick it up. The relief!

Winnie turned her fierce attention to Blair. "Too far!" she said. "That was MEAN." Then she whipped out her wand, waved it, whispered something ... and absolutely nothing happened. Blair grinned triumphantly – she'd got away with it.

Or had she?

"What's going on NOW!" Binxy had come back into the room. "Honestly, you're the worst Year Seven group I've had in years." I had a bad feeling that might be my fault. "Somebody fill me in please... Amara?"

Miss Binx picked on the nearest witch and waggled her wand warningly. "Spill."

Amara shrugged and snitched.

"Explain yourself, Miss Smith-Smythe," said Madam Binx and Blair tried. She really tried.

"It wa—" Blair burped. "B— *Burrp!* B-Bea's fa—" The lie got lost in another loud belch.

"Stop making those disgusting noises and tell me why you took another witch's private journal AND FED IT TO MY PET." Binxy was cross.

"*BURRRRP,*" protested Blair.
"I mean— *BELCH!*"

"You will write a four-hundred-word essay for me comparing the natural and magical diets of giant Venus flytraps and you will have it on my desk by first thing tomorrow morning." Wow, *really* cross.

"B-but, Mad— *Burp!* I—" Blair broke off and stared at Winnie, a look of complete outrage on her face. "Did you SP— *Buuuurrrrrrpppp!*"

Winnie Ross is a GENIUS! It's still making me snigger two days later, possibly because a) Blair was still burping today and b) my diary has finally dried out and (except for the flytrap toothmarks) is as good as new.

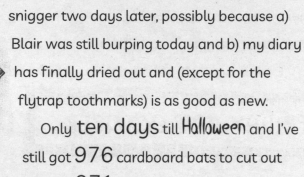

Only **ten days** till **Halloween** and I've still got 976 cardboard bats to cut out (would have been 971 except I accidentally set fire to some of them in Physics).

FRIDAY 22ND OCTOBER

11:10am School

GO is a mad game. I fell down the chimney and when
I rolled out, miraculously in one piece but covered
in soot, all Winnie had to say was that I'd better get
back out there because it was a tight match.

Final score:

DODOS: 99	DRAGONS: 98

Blair is still popping out mini-burps when she least
expects it, which is the only possible excuse for the
SHOCKING FOUL she did on Fabi.

He's covered in cat-shaped plasters but I don't
think he minds too much because WE WON!!

2:55pm

It was Madam Binx's turn to give the Friday lecture and, because of what she referred to as "recent events", her chosen subject was WITCH JOURNALLING. It was, she said with a stern look in the direction of where Year Seven were sitting, an important witch skill that should be treated with *respect*.

"A journal can be not only a written record of your path as a witch, however *bumpy* that path might be –" this time she smiled straight at me – "but a place you can record your thoughts and feelings, especially after rituals or any other special happenings in your magical life. Every witch should have one."

Blair, who was sitting right behind me (which was a shame because I'd been trying very hard to keep out of her way), leaned forwards and whispered in my ear, "Witch journal? Ha! (*tiny burp*) You won't need one of those … just an ORDINARY (*hiccup*) journal for you, Bea Black."

Hunter, who was sitting next to her, laughed.

And after that, even though Binxy was saying lots of really interesting things about mind maps and daily motivations and sticking in cake recipes and autumn leaves, etc. etc., I couldn't concentrate. For someone who never asked to be a witch, I feel surprisingly BAD to be told I'm not one.

The Extraordinary: Halloween Term Issue 2

Sports News and Notices

- After last week's humiliation, Year Seven Dodos are back on <u>winning</u> form against the Dragons. The winning goal in a tight game was scored in extra time by New Girl Bea Black. Well played, Bea!

- Lower Form GOers are reminded that involving the school cats in illegal manoeuvres is very stupid. It will be penalized (if seen) by a two-match suspension. We are all wishing Amara Chukwu a speedy recovery from her severe scratch injuries.

IMPORTANT: Preparations are already underway for the most extraordinary sporting event of the year: the Winter Solstice Grand Tournament! Witches hoping for more THRILLS than SPILLS should start brushing up their broom skills ahead of try-outs next half-term…

Other Notices

Mrs Slater would like to remind all students that the Halloween Ball will end promptly at <u>10pm</u>. There is to be no repetition of last year's post-ball shenanigans.

Quick-fire Q & A with Mr Muddy!

Q: *Favourite meal?*

A: Sausages.

Q: *Favourite teacher?*

A: *Long pause while Mr Muddy blushes and refuses to answer so we're going to say Miss Lupo*

Q: *Favourite joke?*

A: What's it like to be kissed by a vampire? It's a pain in the neck!

Thank you, Mr Muddy! That joke was TERRIBLE.

Dear Agony Witch

Dear Agony Witch,

I'm a new girl and I can't do any magic. I am useless at everything and, although everyone in my class is very kind, I'm sure nobody likes me.

Yours,

A Worried New Girl

I DID NOT WRITE THIS!!!!

8:32pm Home

Three days till Halloween!!!

Very busy day. Had my lunch in the dining room with the rest of the Committee. Obviously, I took in my own food because of my no-witch-food-ever-again rule and, even though they all thought my jam sandwiches were some kind of bloody Halloween prop, they didn't FORCE me to share their sausages.

Jam, not blood.

Spent PD cleaning the Great Chandelier, *again*. It is getting very sparkly and although the spiders are a bit cross about having to move out of our way while we polish, and some of them are very large, I think it's going quite well.

Bat Bunting Tally: 921!!! Mr Zicasso let the whole class help in Art on Tuesday. Blair might not be my FAVOURITE person, but I have to admit she's very quick at cutting out bats. (Hunter said it was a complete accident that he spilled glue on my seat. Sure.)

FRIDAY 29TH OCTOBER

11:03am School

Two days till Halloween!!!!

WILD morning.

Puck said he'd teach me the hair-colour-changing ~~trick~~ spell. I wanted to go temporarily yellow for PE because I'm very committed to being a Dodo, but his ~~demo went wrong.~~ I didn't even have a chance to get my wand out before he'd given me one cat-shaped patch of neon GREEN on my head. He offered to fix it but a) I thought I might end up with no head at all and b) Ms Celery was calling us on to the pitch.

Also ... I don't exactly *hate* it.

Final score:

| DODOS: 190 | DRAGONS: 100 |

Best game ever. I scored SEVEN goals! Puck put it down to the 'lucky cat' on my head. *Obviously*, that had nothing to do with it (but, just in case, I'm keeping it).

5:35pm Home

Dad is freaking out about my hair. He's mostly annoyed that I denied dyeing it, which was not fair because I was actually telling the truth!

"Well, how else did it turn that *interesting* shade?" he asked. I couldn't come up with a fib on the spot, so instead I reminded him he'd said it was good to stand out. That went down as well as could be expected.

5:55pm

Ash came over with some biscuits his mum had baked. I think she worries about us.

I wonder if she'd teach me how to make these

biscuits. They're called koloocheh and they're very pretty but more importantly VERY delicious.

Ash couldn't stop snorting every time he noticed my hair (it's hard to miss).

6:12pm

Koloocheh for tea. Brilliant.

9:33pm

Bat Bunting Tally: *still* 921. Never ever want to see another bat in my life and I've got 279 more to make before lunchtime tomorrow!!

SATURDAY 30TH OCTOBER (HALLOWEEN EVE!!!!!)

3:21pm School

School feels so odd at the weekend! Fewer witches but more cats.

Today's the last day the Junior Committee are allowed into the **Great Hall**. At midnight, the students and teachers on the Senior Ball Committee take over and add what Winnie calls a "few surprises". So we've all been polishing and sweeping and stringing bunting* since DAWN and, not gonna lie, I think we've done an AMAZING job. The hall is SPARKLING, with every single cobweb intact. All the polished cake stands and shiny punchbowls have been delivered back to Sir Scary Cook, Zephyr's gold

---

*1,188 bats, which is close enough for even Winnie to be pleased.

throne is by the fireplace and the Great Chandelier is blinding! But we're all FILTHY and STARVING so we're off to Taffy Tallywick's to recover.

8:50pm Home

Nervous but also more excited about the party tomorrow than I thought I would be. I hope everyone likes the bunting. As long as nobody forces me to dance, it should be fine.

I've got the weirdest feeling I'm forgetting something I should be worrying about...

SUNDAY 31ST OCTOBER (HALLOWEEEEENNNNN!!!!!)

5:01pm Home

"Ta-da!" says Dad. "Look what I made!"

I don't say anything, mostly because my jaw is on the floor.

"It's for YOU!"

NOOOOOOOO! I've remembered what I should have been worrying about. My costume.

"Stop scribbling in that diary for once and say something!"

Er...

5:15pm

"It's ... WOW!" I managed at last. "It's so GREEN!"

Dad nodded happily. It was VERY green.

"It's a FROG!" He was so proud. "Because I know how much you like them."

I gulped – 'it' was a very BIG, *suspiciously spacehopper-sized* FROG costume. Dad set it down on the floor and, with a flourish, produced a bright green T-shirt and a pair of tights, neon-green face paint and some goggly, froggy eyes *boinging* around on a headband. "The finishing touches!"

He was not wrong. I was FINISHED.

"And I know it's not *anatomically correct*," he said, as if the rest was, "but I added a handy pouch to the front for snacks or whatever you carry around with you ... a hairbrush? Lipgloss?"

A hairbrush wasn't going to help. *Lipgloss* wasn't going to help! To be fair, snacks might. Where were the emergency biscuits?

6:21pm

I am standing by my bed, DESPAIRING. I would be lying face down on my bed, DESPAIRING, if it wasn't for the sad fact that I *can't* lie down.

I am IN the frog costume. I am *Bea-frogged*.

What. Am. I. Going. To. Do? This is one of the most serious and terrible crises of my entire life (which is why, even in the DEPTHS of my despair, I am writing it all down).

If I wear this costume, it will mean social death.

But if I don't wear it, I might make Dad CRY.

6:25pm

Through my sweaty panic, I could vaguely hear someone calling my name and a second later a football *WHOOSHED* through my open window. Ash was trying to get my attention. I'd definitely got *his* attention – he had tears running down his face.

"It is NOT FUNNY!" I yelled, lobbing the ball back and narrowly missing him. Shame.

"It sort of *is*," he snorted. He laughed so much he nearly fell out of the window (which would have served him right). "Have fun though!" he shouted and grinned, and I couldn't help but grin back even though IT IS NOT FUNNY.

6:32pm

Right. I have a solution.

I will leave the house in Full Frog and get changed in the forest. I can hide some leggings in the pouch, *and diary too!* although even if I had to go to the ball in my underwear that would be an improvement.

6:38pm

Dad is driving me to school! He is being completely UNREASONABLE – no matter what I say I can't persuade him to let me walk through the forest in the dark dressed as a frog.

My life is over.

7:13pm School

I'm having a little moment in a cupboard while I calm down. The last five minutes have been TRAUMATIC.

We pulled up in front of the school and Dad (who was overexcited because there was a minor meteor shower over the chimneys) *rolled me* off the back seat like a … well, spacehopper. Sadly, we were not alone. There were orange bubble cars everywhere dropping off witches. Witches ready to party, witches in perfect costumes that can only be achieved with some serious wand-work … witches in perfect *witch costumes…*

Nooooooo.

Slinky witches and fluorescent witches and witches in saris, crinoline-wearing witches with pointy hats and witches in velvet flares and witches in head-to-toe black Lycra with stripes on their capes. Everyone was wearing black – shiny black or glittery black or black with feathers, but only black. Even all the cats were black. There were witches on roller skates and witches on stilts. *There was even a small witch in a ragged cloak with very realistic warts.*

What there wasn't was a single witch-as-a-FROG
– or witch-as-anything-but-witch. And nobody was
green.

Dad and I looked at each other. "Oh well," he said
with a guilty shrug, turning the key in the ignition.
"It's good to stand out." And then he was off!

He wasn't the only one who made a speedy
getaway. I took one look at the growing crowd of
witches-as-witches, pointing and *ooh*ing at me, and
ran as fast as I could – not that fast in this costume –
to the nearest available broom cupboard.

7:17pm

Wait, I've got my wand in my pouch! This would be a
really good time to discover if I can finally do magic…

7:21pm

OK, I still can't do magic, but I now have a small
singed hole in the middle of my massive frog bum
and I've eaten all my snacks.

I'm not having a good time.

7:23pm

Maybe I could steal one of these broomsticks and fly away to somewhere like the Galapagos Islands (??) where they might appreciate human-sized frogs? No one will miss m——

11:29pm Home
SPOILER! The Halloween Ball is over and I'm still alive.

It was Winnie and Puck who came to get me. They nearly fell over at the FROGGINESS of me, but they recovered quickly and then literally took the pen out of my hand and *dragged* me out of the broom cupboard.

"You're not missing tonight, Boa," said Winnie so fiercely that several of the floofy things decorating her witch's hat fell off.

"Wouldn't be the same without you, Hoppy!" shouted Puck, tugging me in the direction of the party, the music getting louder as we approached.

Oh my broomstick! Being on the Junior Ball Committee had not prepared me for THIS!

"*Apple and toffee?*" Unless I was going mad,*
two of the silvery birch trees that usually
stood at the entrance to the school had
... somehow ... *relocated* to stand at
the entrance to the **Great Hall**
and were ... *serving drinks.* "*Or
strudel and coffee?*" The nearest
tree adjusted one of the bow ties
attached to his lower branches.
"U-u-mm, apple and
t-toffee?' I stammered and
he ladled punch from a bowl
hanging off another of his
branches into a small red crystal glass.
"*Happy Halloween!*" He presented the cup to me
with a flourish and ushered me into the hall. "*I'm sure
it will be a night to remember.*" He was not wrong.
It was like walking into a CAULDRON!**
The Great Chandelier was gleaming and
glimmering with zillions of tiny red candles, and the

*Not impossible..
**IN A GOOD WAY!!

spiders we'd very carefully not dusted away were busy weaving and re-weaving their silk threads in intricate patterns between the layers of lights so that new pictures constantly appeared and disappeared in shadows on the walls – leaping cats and duelling vampires and prancing unicorns and more!

A DJ booth was floating on a magic carpet above the dance floor, surrounded by glittering disco balls twirling in mid-air. Behind the decks, Mr Muddy in a scary-scientist-witch costume, assisted by Indiana Bones, was busting out 'Thriller'.

In one corner of the hall, some crab apples were fluttering about on tiny leaf wings ("the witch version of apple bobbing," explained Puck) and on the other side of the room a small gaggle of witches and their cats were toasting marshmallows over one of the flaming torches attached to the wall.

Up above, the bat bunting, *my bat bunting*, was hanging in loops criss-crossing the ceiling, swaying gently in a breeze no one could feel, so that it really did look like they were flying! Not gonna lie: I felt PROUD, but ... while *I* might be looking at strings of paper bats, I was suddenly *very* aware that everyone else was looking at *me*.

There were at least a hundred costumed witches in here and I was *still* the only FROG. There were *actual* frogs of course – the class frogs were doing an acrobatics display on a golden table under the chandelier and Stan, hiding at the back, was looking from the costume to me, and back again, with a look of HORROR on his little froggy face.

"I'm sorry," I mouthed at him, trying to ignore the fact I was now surrounded by a small crowd of pointing witches.

"Wow!" It was Hunter's voice. I had literally stopped a conga in its tracks. "That is *some* costume." I had a feeling that was not a

compliment. Hunter poked me in my papier-mâché stomach. "WOW!" he said again. "I don't know how you did it, but ... *cool*."

Then someone started to clap. And, one by one, all the other witches – in their annoyingly perfect WITCH costumes – joined in.

I was DEAD.

"That. Is. Amazing." Fabi broke out of the conga line and loped over. "And it matches your hair! What spell did you use?"

I mumbled that I hadn't spelled it, that my dad had made it.

There was a collective *gasp*.

"He MADE it?!" Fabi's eyes widened. "Like, with his *hands*? And, like, not a *wand*?"

I went red under the green face paint and shook my head.

"No magic at all?" Hunter raised one eyebrow. "I don't believe you."

"Is he an artist?" whispered a small witch in a

black lace cape, with a glittery witch's hat over her headscarf.

"So cool, so *avant-garde*." Mr Zicasso (in black sequins) had whizzed over now and was considering me from every angle like I was an original work by Da Vinciwick.

"And there's a pouch!" squealed Madam Binx, floating over to have a closer look. "I do love a costume with pockets."

"You're the first witch who's come as something other than A WITCH for a hundred and thirty-three years." Gilbert Swizz, *the actual head boy*, sauntered over and nodded approvingly, sending a ripple of impressed whispers round the crowd. *Approvingly?*

Wait ... it was dawning on me ... my costume was a HIT!

"Would your dad make one for me next year?" asked a random Year Ten.

"Can he do any other animals?" asked another. "Like an elephant?"

"A slow-worm?"

"A duck-billed platypus?" Suggestions were coming thick and fast.

"An axolotl?" That was Puck.

I nodded manically, goggly eyes boinging around on my head.

"Right, witches!" Mr Muddy came out from behind the decks. "Let Bea sample the delights of her first Halloween Ball!"

"Dance with us, Bea!" Amara (who had gone full witchy witch with long golden chin hairs and *stripey socks*) was already pulling me towards the throng of witches in the middle of the room.

"Maybe later?" I hung back. Unless I was alone in the forest in the dark, I found dancing *challenging* and they all seemed to know the complicated steps to a song I'd never heard before.

"Cakes then," Amara said happily and, before I knew what I was doing, we were heading at speed – Puck and Winnie and Fabi too – towards a long table at the side of the hall set with our 107 gleaming, towering cake stands, the 33 punchbowls, candelabras, flowers and glimmering crystals and surrounded by a little crowd already munching away. Everyone looked happy enough, but what I wanted to know was *why was there smoke coming out of their noses and ears??*

Puck grabbed what looked like a red velvet cupcake and took a huge bite. **POOOOFFFFF!** Little puffs of sparkly blue steam shot out of his ears. Winnie took a big bite out of what might have been a brownie. **WHOOSH!** Red steam puffed out of her nostrils. She giggled.

"Try one, Bea!"

Nooooooo, not witch food!

But Puck was already advancing with a cupcake and before I could duck my mouth was full of— OH! The first bite tasted like the crispiest apple but as soon as I swallowed there was a loud **PUFF**, my ears were streaming green smoke and the bite of cake burst into the most delicious warm liquid toffee I'd ever tasted in my life!

But, at the exact moment I was falling in love with **Witch Halloween**, the doors to the hall burst open and Izzi appeared, walking backwards. "BEHOLD, the **QUEEEN of MISCHIEFFFFF** is in the house!" she announced.

Blair Smith-Smythe pushed a trio of Year Eights out of the way and struck a *serious* pose in the doorway. She was wearing the most *extra* **Halloween** costume I'd ever seen in my entire life. And *I* was green and about two metres in diameter.

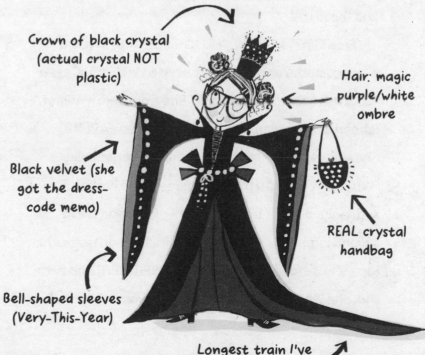

Crown of black crystal (actual crystal NOT plastic)

Hair: magic purple/white ombre

Black velvet (she got the dress-code memo)

REAL crystal handbag

Bell-shaped sleeves (Very-This-Year)

Longest train I've ever seen

She cracked out of her pose at last and sashayed into the middle of the room. "Happy Halloween, witches!" She gave a little twirl. "Now your queen has arrived, I guess it's time to get this party STARTED!"

"Um, Blair," Fabi snorted. "I think this party has *already* started."

"Yeah," a very cool Year Ten joined in. "It started when Frog Girl arrived!"

Everyone turned to look at me (AGAIN). I gulped. Blair swivelled, very slowly, on her bejewelled heel and faced me.

"Frog Girl?" she spat. "FROG GIRL? *That's* NOT a witch costume and *she* is not even a WITCH, far less a Halloween Queen! What's this?" She flounced over and jabbed at my green belly. "Paper? Green PAPER?!" She swooshed her silk cloak around dramatically. "What sort of **toadbrain** wears—" She broke off suddenly, clasped her hand to her forehead and a second later the smuggest of smirks spread across her face. "Oh, whatever – it's time for MISCHIEF!" and with that she whipped out her wand and pointed it at ME...

"With style already wishy-washy,
Make this costume squishy-squashy!"

But, just as she flicked her wand, Puck appeared from nowhere and yelled, "NOT HOPPY!" and rugby-tackled her from behind! They both crashed to the floor. Blair's wand tumbled out of her grip and arched upwards through the air, spinning and somersaulting and shooting a chaotic trail of purple sparks towards the ceiling.

Magic on the loose!

There was a rustling, a *rrippppp* and then ... *squealing*. Very nervously, I looked up. *BATS...*

Swooping and diving, so many bats, landing on so many cats and on so many witchy hats. One whole string was down – *a hundred bats!*

My bat bunting was coming to life!

Real ex-bat-bunting bats are *HYPER*. Just like Puck had warned. I'd never seen such an overexcited, giddy, sniggering bunch of flappers in my life.

Oh no – another string was down! And another! It was like the runaway magic was leaping from string to string ... *hundreds* of bats circling the ceiling in a whirlpool of black wings, sending the Great Chandelier swinging! They streamed round the room as disco balls dropped from the ceiling, one of the serving trees fainted with a great crash and a flurry of leaves and students scattered out of their way, knocking over tables piled high with food as they went and—

Eeeeeurgh! I had a BAT IN MY HAIR!

Ms Sparks sprang into action first, pulling out her wand. "Contain them!" she yelled, looking around wildly. "Keep them away from the drinks!"

But it was too late – they'd made a beeline (batline?) for the punch and drained the bowls in seconds – if they'd been

overexcited before, now on a complete sugar high the bats were out of control! And they weren't the only ones – half of us were yelling and screaming and shaking mini vampires out of our hair and cloaks.

Teachers pushed their way through the panicking crowds, fumbling for their wands. "Don't let them near the cakes!" shouted one. Again, too late – a battalion of bats was trailing streamers of coloured smoke like the Red Arrows.

"Into the FIREPLACE!" yelled the head and a herd of obedient witches tumbled towards the grate, sending Zephyr and her golden throne flying. "Not you lot – the BATS! Steer them into the fireplace and up and out of the chimney!"

Under Ms Sparks's instruction, all the teachers stopped panicking and swept into the centre of the dance floor, flicking their wands and incanting in perfect unison. The Year Elevens joined the fray too, jumping over younger years and pulling cleverly concealed wands from their elaborate costumes. The chanting grew louder and louder until the walls were shaking.

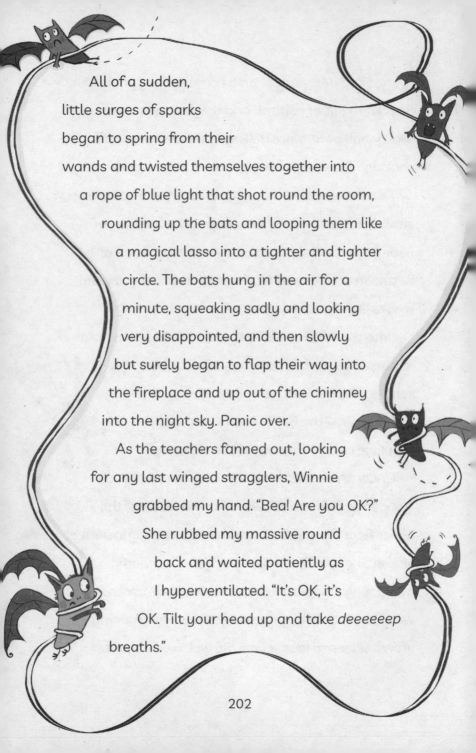

All of a sudden,
little surges of sparks
began to spring from their
wands and twisted themselves together into
a rope of blue light that shot round the room,
rounding up the bats and looping them like
a magical lasso into a tighter and tighter
circle. The bats hung in the air for a
minute, squeaking sadly and looking
very disappointed, and then slowly
but surely began to flap their way into
the fireplace and up out of the chimney
into the night sky. Panic over.

As the teachers fanned out, looking
for any last winged stragglers, Winnie
grabbed my hand. "Bea! Are you OK?"
She rubbed my massive round
back and waited patiently as
I hyperventilated. "It's OK, it's
OK. Tilt your head up and take *deeeeeep*
breaths."

I did as she said and that was when I saw it – *one stray baby bat nibbling through the red silk rope that held up the chandelier!* He was right down to the very last few threads, gnashing as fast as he could, and the whole chandelier was swinging and twisting violently RIGHT ABOVE THE FROG TABLE.

Visions of flying frogs' legs and frogs' arms and all their other froggy bits flashed before my eyes. The chandelier's candles were flickering and starting to go out, spiders were clinging on like it was the *Titanic* and if it fell witches might get hurt too!

Before I'd even thought about what I was doing, I had grabbed my wand out of my pouch and pointed it at the chandelier, *willing* it to stay UP. My hand was shaking (or was it the wand quivering?) as another thread snapped and the chandelier jolted, it was coming down! Stan was going to get SQUASHED!

Wishing beyond wishing, I focused as hard as I could and then, by ~~some miracle some magic~~ *my magic*, the chandelier ... STOPPED and just *hung*

there, twirling slower
and slower like a big
glowing planet in
the sky.

Everyone turned
to stare up at it. Ms
Sparks looked at me,
then at my wand, then
back at me. "Well done,
Bea!" she gasped, rushing
over. "You can relax – we've got it
now." Gently, she took the wand out of my hand.

"Was it really *me* that stopped it?" I held my
breath.

Ms Sparks smiled and told me it really, *really* was,
that I'd been the only one who'd even seen what was
happening. And then she said she'd always known I
could do it.

Seriously? *I* hadn't.

"But I'm *ordinary*," I said and she shrugged in a so-
what kind of way. "I'm NOT A WITCH," I tried again.

She laughed and pointed at the chandelier that was even now being rehung on new red ropes as a result of some nifty wand-weaving by Binxy and Miss Lupo. "Er, I think you are. How else do you explain what just happened?" I didn't know what to say. "Also, you have a decidedly witchy kinship with frogs." I looked down at Stan who had hopped on to my big green belly.

"Maybe just this one?" I said and she laughed. "But I'm not from an extraordinary family." I said it again, louder this time – it didn't matter if they all heard because they all already knew. "I'm an *Ordinary*."

"*Pfffff!*" Ms Sparks flapped her hand like she was swatting away a fly. "Oh, me too."

Whaaaaaattttt?!

"Nothing to be ashamed of. It doesn't matter where you start, it's where you end up that counts." Zephyr, perched safely on her shoulder again, nodded. "Hard work and belief, that's all it takes – not that that's easy." And then Ms Sparks told me, loud enough so everyone standing nearby could hear, including Blair who was looking nervous next to a very angry Mr Muddy, that she was really PROUD of me.

"It wasn't Blair's fault," I said, suddenly feeling bad. "She was only doing a Queen of Mischief spell."

Ms Sparks raised an eyebrow and gave Blair a long look. "Halloween mischief should never be directed at one singled-out witch," she said sternly but, before Blair could say anything, Puck spoke up.

"It was MY fault really," he said. "It all went a bit wrong." He looked at me and mumbled, "Sorry. I was trying to help."

I grinned at him – I knew that.

"Well," said Ms Sparks slowly, "it certainly made for a memorable Halloween. Mistakes," she looked from Blair to Puck and back again, "were certainly made, but I don't suppose there's much that can't be fixed with an advanced tidying-up spell." We all took a moment to look around at the smashed disco balls, upturned chairs, discarded costumes and squashed cakes. "No real harm done – thanks to Bea!"

I went red again and looked at Winnie and Fabi and Amara and Puck.

"I had help," I said and picked a fat spider out of my hair.

"Didn't someone say something about getting this party started? *Again*." Mr Muddy was grinning at Ms Sparks. And, on the count of three, they both flicked out their wands and, in less time than it takes me to eat a fluffmallow, everything was the right way up, the punchbowls were refilling themselves, the candles were bursting back into flame and the disco balls were floating into place.

"DJ Bones on the decks!" shouted Indiana, restarting the music, and with one more swish of Ms Sparks's wand, little glowing stars strung themselves across the ceiling where the bat bunting had been. "Much safer!" She winked at me, but before I could reply, Fabi and Amara and Winnie and Puck had grabbed me and pulled me on to the packed dance floor.

BEST PARTY EVER.

Afterwards, it took me quite a while to get to the car because a) I had to frog-hop and b) I had to say goodbye to everyone because I won't see them until after half-term. Well, except I *will* see Winnie and Puck and Fabi and Amara because we're going to meet at Taffy Tallywick's tomorrow for a major post-party gossip!

"Here," said Winnie as I was about to go. She held out a slightly squished Halloween cake. "It was the last one left and we all thought you deserved it the most."

Oh! I took it carefully and concentrated on the tiny bat-teeth marks in the icing so I wouldn't get TEARY.

"The magic should wear off in about an hour," explained Fabi, "but it will still taste amazing."

I nodded and mumble-thanked them and we all HUGGED (well, as much as we could given my frogginess and without squashing the cake any more).

"So?" Dad asked as he rolled me on to the back seat. "Did you have fun?"

I said I'd had **SOOOOOOOOOOOOO MUCH FUN** but after a minute of babble about toffee smoke and bunting I *stopped*... There was so much I was never going to be able to tell him, however much I wanted to! But for once Dad wasn't nagging me for details – he couldn't wait to tell *me* something.

"I was going to wait until tomorrow, but maybe this is the right moment."

"What?" I asked, looking at the roof of the car and wishing I could scratch my real tummy.

"It came." He was being very mysterious.

"*What* came?"

"Guess," he said.

I had a head full of Halloween magic and I was *very* uncomfortable and needed a wee. This was no time for guessing games. "Just *tell* me."

So he blurted it out. "They've accepted you."

"Who?" I asked.

"The **Academy** of course."

It still took me a minute to work out what he was talking about.

The **Academy**, with its shiny new buildings and its football teams and sensible uniform and sensible everything. Oh. *Oh*.

"B-but," I began as we drew up outside our house. I was still but-butting when two minutes later in the kitchen he handed me the letter.

Mr Black
1 Piggoty Lane
Little Spellshire
Spellshire

SPELLSHIRE ACADEMY

Finding the Excellence in the Ordinary

30th October

Dear Mr Black,

Further to our letter dated 7th October, we are now pleased to inform you that we can make a place available to Miss Bea Black from Monday 8th November (return date from half-term).

Please confirm Miss Black's acceptance in writing.

Yours faithfully,

Dr S. N. Sibbel

Admissions

I *tried* a happy smile.

"You wanted this, right?" Dad was looking at me very closely.

"The thing is," I began. "The thing is..." I scrambled out of my green shell and sat down at the table in my tights and T-shirt. For what I was about to tell him, I really needed to be less FROGGY. "I ... er ... the thing is ... um..." He was putting me off by staring at me in a very intense Dad-looking-right-inside-me kind of way. "The thing is ... Winnie and Puck and—" I broke off again. I wasn't entirely sure where I was going with this. "Well, Extraordinary, it's not so..." I shrugged.

"You haven't, by any chance, changed your mind about something?"

I nodded.

"Let me guess – you don't want to go to the Academy any more?"

I nodded again and flakes of green face paint fell on to the table.

"You want to stay at Extraordinary?"

This time I nodded so hard my eyes fell off.[*]

---

[*] Not my ACTUAL eyes, my frog eyes.

"Well –" Dad popped a couple of wonky slices of bread in the toaster – "I always say being open to changing your mind is an underrated skill." He waggled his eyebrows at me and I grinned – that was one of his very favourite things to say. "Good decision, Bea Black," Dad said and burned the toast.

11:44pm

The first thing I did when I came upstairs was open my window and YELL and, seconds later, a sleepy-looking Ash opened *his* window and grinned over at me.

"Good party?" he shouted and I shouted back that it was absolutely BRILLIANT and then – because I could hardly give him any witchy details – I lobbed over the leftover Halloween cake.

"That. Is. The. *MOST. AMAZINGEST.* Thing. I've. EVER. Tasted!" he yelled through the crumbs, but then his mum came in to tell him to stop shouting and especially to stop insulting her cooking and go back to bed.

I was the only person who noticed the tiniest wisp of green smoke coming out of his nostrils!

~~11:59pm~~ Midnight

I didn't see it until I was getting into bed – a parcel tied up in brown paper and string tucked under the covers...

A brand-new DIARY exactly like this one except less dog-eared!

Happy Halloween, Bea! I thought you might be needing this! Dad xx

There's just enough space left in this one for one last list...

Things I Will ACHIEVE Next Half-Term Now I Have Friends

- Master all the trickiest GO skills including the Flying Cat Swerve and the Boggle Dodge.
- Persuade Dad to buy me a puppy (also ask if I can stay on frog rota because of STAN).
- Be the best vice-captain of the Dodos since the time of Minerva Moon.
- Find out who Minerva Moon is was.
- Learn to cook/make potions/bake.
- Ask Blair to teach me how to do the loop-the-loop on my broom.
- Levitate STUFF!

YEAR SEVEN CLASS PHOTO

ABOUT THE AUTHOR*

Bea Black is eleven years old and has recently
moved to Little Spellshire where she lives with
her dad, a weather scientist. She has no pets,
but has been on class frog rota this half-term.
Her lifelong dream is to get a puppy.
This is Bea's first diary.

*With a bit of help from Perdita and Honor Cargill!